Stolen By The Pack

OMEGA FOR THE PACK
BOOK ONE

LAYLA SPARKS

SAPPHIRE INK PUBLISHING

Omegaverse Terms

A few things to know regarding the omegaverse world. The people in the omegaverse display a canine or wolflike behavior. Some books involve shifting into wolves. This series will have minimal shifting.

Here are some terms that will be helpful to know (*note: these definitions pertain to my stories):

Omega: A female or male who would often have multiple partners to help them during heats. Usually has a particular scent that alphas find very appealing and unable to resist.

Beta: Like a normal human but in the wolf world

Alpha: Top of the food chain, and they gravitate to omegas. They also have a scent to attract omegas.

Delta: Ferocious and deadly, typically guards and second in command to alphas

Slick: Secretion from the privates

Heat: A period where an omega needs to mate - akin to ovulating in human females.

Knot: When an alpha mates an omega— and the base of the penis swells, locking the alpha and omega in place

Rut: Alphas can go into rut phase, similar to heat. Sometimes an omega's heat will bring it on.

Scent blockers: Can come in pills or as a cream. Blocks an omega scent from attracting alphas.

Heat Suppressants: Stops an omega from going into heat

Content Guide

~ Double Penetration

    ~ Menage

    ~ Group Play

    ~ Backdoor (anal) Play

    ~ Kidnapping

    ~ Pregnancy

    ~ Domestic Discipline/ Spanking

    ~ Claiming bites

For readers who prefer not to read about pregnancy or babies, please skip Chapter 21-Epilogue.

Prologue

Bianca

I breathed out a sigh of relief after having to push all night long. Sweat trickled down my face as we heard the small cry of a baby.

"It's a girl!" announced the midwife.

My husband, Therman, squeezed my hand, and I smiled, seeing pride and shock in his eyes as he gazed at our little girl. The midwife walked across the room, and I could hear our baby's little cries as the midwife washed her up and measured her.

My eyes were glued to our little bundle, my heart hurting at her cries. My physical pain and discomfort were forgotten at the moment as we stared at our little baby.

"You did it, honey," Therman praised, kissing me on the forehead.

The midwife laid the baby on my chest, and my heart swelled with admiration for her. In my dreams leading up to the birth, I knew the baby was going to be a girl. And she was finally here.

I touched her little shoulder carefully. Her wrinkly purple skin was so soft against mine. She calmed down instantly and stopped crying at my touch.

"Her name will be Tiana," I cooed.

"She's perfect," my husband agreed, placing his finger in her palm. Tiana's fingers closed over his, and Therman smiled widely.

"She has the mark," said the midwife, pointing to a pink mark on my baby's shoulder. I panicked as I quickly looked at her shoulder. It looked like four claw marks. "It's the omega sign. She's an omega. I couldn't see it at first until you held her."

Omegas were rare and highly coveted in our community in Howl's Edge. They were distinguishable by the mark on their shoulder, signifying they belonged to a pack later in their lives.

"How is that possible?" I asked in shock.

I turned to my husband, whose eyes were as wide as mine.

"Well, it makes sense. I'm an alpha, even though you're a beta. It's rare, but it happens," Therman assured me. "We have to leave Howl's Edge immediately. Before anyone takes our child."

Horror filled my heart at the thought of anyone taking my baby. It wasn't safe during these times.

She could get kidnapped off the street or sent to the Omega Auctions. We weren't wealthy enough to protect her on the island. No matter how they obtained her, it was the law for an omega to mate with alphas. She would be taken by alphas and made to mate with three or more of them. I couldn't let that happen.

"We have to leave tonight," I said, trying to get up, but my head spun.

"Miss, you just gave birth," insisted the midwife.

"We will take the first boat out in a couple of days,"

assured Therman. He kissed our daughter's head and rubbed my arm reassuringly. "I'll make sure our family is safe. Whatever it takes."

One

TIANA

Twenty-Four Years Later

I stared at the pill bottle sitting in front of the mirror with dread.

I always dreaded taking the unknown pills, but then I'd hear my mom's voice in the back of my head, *"You need to take these every day, Tiana. Do you hear me? Every day or else something bad will happen."*

I was all dressed to go partying with my friend Lori in ten minutes, and she was arriving soon to pick me up from my parents' house. I snapped on rose gold earrings to match my gold dress, which clung to my curves and stopped just above my knees. My cleavage showed quite a bit in this dress, and I pulled it up a little bit in case my mother threw a fit.

Even though I was twenty-four, my parents were still highly protective of me, and I had no idea why. It had been that way ever since I was a baby. They always claimed that I wasn't like the other girls and that I was *special*.

Whatever the hell that meant.

Picking up the bottle of pills, I turned the bottle around

"]

to look for a label or anything on it like I always did to find out what it was. As usual, there was nothing there. Opening the bottle, I poured out a pill filled with translucent gray matter floating inside, which sat on my palm. I stared at it in disgust. I only really started questioning what the pills were when I hit my late teens.

My parents were secretive, claiming that they were vitamins, but my mom had a lifetime supply of them under her bed for me. Vitamins had labels, names, and lots of numbers.

This bottle had nothing to indicate what it was.

So, instead of taking the pill this time, I walked to the toilet and flushed it down. I wasn't going to take something that I wasn't sure of anymore. If my parents cared enough, they'd tell me what it was for. I felt a sort of victory watching it disappear while anxiety rippled through my stomach. I had never directly disobeyed them like this, but I was getting fed up with the half-assed answers and bullshit.

Grabbing my small purse, I slung it over my shoulder and headed across the tiny hallway of our apartment into the living room, where my parents were hanging out after their shifts together at a retail store across the street. They were lounging on the old couch, which had tufts of cotton sticking out, and quietly chatted while watching the evening news.

"Tiana, where are you going?" Mom asked, looking at me inquisitively and pushing up her large-rimmed glasses. She was like a hawk, constantly watching everything I did.

"Just going out with my friend," I said vaguely, stepping into my black heels and strapping them on.

"You look like you're going to party or something. What's the big occasion?"

"We just need a break from college life. That's all there is to it, Mom," I sighed, getting fed up with her line of questioning. She got especially nervous if I was around guys or if I mentioned a guy in particular. This was her way to prevent me from ever dating. Her reason was that I needed to finish college first before getting into a relationship.

"Don't have too much fun," chuckled Dad, cracking a peanut shell with his teeth.

I just wanted to scream that I could have all the fun if I wanted to, but I held it back.

"Yeah, I won't," I said, leaving out the front door before either of them could say another word. Thankfully, Lori was pulling up at the side of the road at that moment. My heels clicked on the cracked cement sidewalk, and I nearly tripped several times over the uneven road.

"Hey!" said Lori as I got into the car.

"Hey," I greeted back, sighing when I pulled the seatbelt.

"What's wrong, girlie?"

"Nothing," I said. "It just sucks to still live with the parents. You know?"

"Haha, yeah, that sounds terrible," she said, flipping her curly blond hair back. She wore a tie-dye print dress that was unique but also stylish paired with lime green heels. Her several keys jangled in the ignition along with a sizeable pink fur teddy bear attached to it.

"I'm so ready to party," said Lori. "It might make me stop thinking of terrible James and the migraine from classes. My god."

"I need to get out too," I agreed, watching the road as she took a left turn to the bar she was heading to. It was the liveliest bar in Seattle, with plenty of cute guys and action. Low-key, I was hoping to meet a guy and finally have an adventure of my own. But for some reason, it was tough for me to get excited about a relationship, and I've never met a man who could give me butterflies.

"I have something to ask you. A favor," said Lori.

"Yeah?"

"Well, umm. This is sort of last minute," said Lori. I knew

full well she was going to ask, regardless. She was crazy like that. "My cousin invited me to her cruise ship, and I was wondering if you'd like to come with me. I can bring one other person, and it's all paid for."

Oh no, my parents would lose their minds if I ever slept anywhere else but at home.

"I don't think..."

"I know, Tiana. Even when we were kids, you were never allowed to come to sleepovers with me or anything," sighed Lori. "But you're fucking twenty-four, for goodness sake. Why can't you distance yourself from your family a little bit? Live your own life?"

"What if I didn't want to go?" I asked, taking offense that she'd jump to conclusions so quickly, even though she was right.

"I highly doubt that," said Lori. "This is a cruise vacation. Three days."

"When is it? I need to make sure I'm not busy or anything."

"It's the day after tomorrow. Sunday," said Lori.

"Whoa, that's super short notice," I said. "I don't know."

"Before you write it off, please think about it," said Lori. "I really need you. My cousin is a catty bitch, and I need someone there. I don't have any fucking friends except for you."

Ugh, when she put it like *that*....

"Fine, I'll think about it," I said as she parked the car in front of the establishment. It was already crowded with people at 8 pm, surprisingly. Friday nights were busy, and I gulped with nervousness. I never enjoyed going out partying with Lori, but I needed to get out of my comfort zone.

And not be so scared of what my parents would think.

Just a couple of hours later, I was already tired of partying. The music was blasting as I tried to talk loudly enough for Lori to hear.

"What are you saying?" shouted Lori for the fifth time, drink in hand and very wobbly.

"You're not supposed to be drinking. You're driving us back," I said, but it looked hopeless now. I wouldn't trust her to drive at this point at all. She was already extra giggly with the guys and didn't seem stable to me.

"You can drive my car," she said as another guy handed her a shot, and she gulped it down.

Shit. I didn't have a license, and she knew it. I only had my driver's permit, but I had never gotten around to getting my license. As a college student, I couldn't afford a car yet and planned to get one when I got a real job. And there's no way my parents had time to teach me to drive since they were always working.

While I contemplated what to do, a guy approached me as I sipped on water.

"Let me buy you a drink, pretty lady," he said.

"No, thanks," I said. "I may need to drive today."

"Ah, got you," he said. Then he slowly veered away from me. No one wanted to party with someone who wasn't drinking. I was just a little too boring for this place, but someone needed to be the responsible one. Two hours being here was more than enough, and I wanted to leave. No guy here intrigued me enough to talk, and Lori was surrounded.

I grabbed her wrist and started tugging her towards the door.

"Noo, I'm not ready to leave!" she slurred, setting her glass on the bar counter on our way out.

"I know, but it's getting late," I said.

"You're just scared of your parents," she said snidely once we were outside. Anger rose in my chest, but I knew she was super drunk, and there was nothing to gain by fighting with her. I'd have a rational conversation with her tomorrow.

"No, I'm not," I said. "Let's get you to your stupid car."

"At least I have a car," she said. *God*, she was combative when she was drunk.

"But you're too drunk to drive it," I said. "Give me your keys."

She floundered as she dug into her purse and shakily handed it to me. I was going to have to drive, that was for sure. I would have to sleep at her place until she could drop me off tomorrow. I crashed at her place a few times before, so I didn't mind that. We were like sisters.

After making sure she was settled in the backseat, I hopped into the driver's seat. My heart pounded hard as I twisted the key into the ignition. Lori had shown me a couple of times how to drive, so it wasn't like I didn't have a clue of what I was doing. I wasn't one hundred percent confident, though.

"Keep your foot on the brake," said Lori, now more alert since her life was in potential danger in my hands.

I backed the car out, looking over my shoulder a million times. I didn't want to accidentally murder anyone tonight. For a split second, I wondered what would happen if I did. I shuddered with relief when I finally backed the car out of the parking lot and was on the road. I was driving way under the speed limit since there weren't many cars around.

"I think I'm getting the hang of this," I said, trying to keep the car centered on the road.

"Thank goodness," sighed Lori. Through my rearview mirror, I saw her lean back and close her eyes. But looking at my rearview mirror for that couple of seconds was a big mistake. When I heard the sound of metal crashing and twisting, I snapped my gaze back.

I crashed into the stop sign. I quickly slammed on the brakes, and Lori flew forward, grabbing onto my seat.

"What the fuck?" she shouted, looking at the damaged sign on the ground.

I was panicking as I looked around. It was nighttime, and cars were still going down the road like nothing happened. Suddenly police sirens and a loud voice on the intercom sounded behind us for me to pull over.

"Shit," I said as I pulled over to the side of the road.

"We're in so much fucking trouble," said Lori.

The cop walked over to the car and knocked on my window. My finger was shaking as I pressed the button to roll the window down. He rested his large muscular arm on the frame of the window, and he was so tall that I couldn't see his face.

"Step out of your car, ma'am."

I unlocked the car and carefully stepped out, leaving the door open behind me with my hands raised in the air.

"Sorry about that stop sign. It won't happen again," I said shakily. The cop towered above me, his muscular frame was visible underneath his uniform- upper arms bulging from his vest. The thing that struck me the most was his eyes. The golden flecks in his iris made my heart pound faster, and adrenaline shot through me. I had never felt like this with any guy before.

Ever. And from my nervousness, I was sweating profusely, and the smell of strawberries was emanating from me. It was like someone had bathed me in strawberry shampoo. *What the hell was happening to me?*

"The stop sign will survive," he said with a hint of a hard smile. "I'm here to make sure everyone's okay. May I see your license?"

I went back into the car, and Lori was sitting there with wide eyes.

"He wants my freaking license," I whispered harshly to her as I pretended to rummage in the compartment.

"Oh fuck," muttered Lori.

After having wasted enough time pretending, I pulled back from the car, ready to confess.

"No license?" he inquired before I could speak.

I shook my head.

Two

GRANT

I thought this would be a normal night of being on patrol and stopping random people on the road. But this traffic stop was turning out to be way more abnormal than I thought. This was no ordinary girl.

As she stood in front of me trembling, my nostrils flared at her delicious strawberry scent.

She was clearly an omega. And I wondered why the fuck she was here and not in Howl's Edge. I wasn't aware of omegas starting their own colony elsewhere without alphas unless she was the lost omega.

The one I was looking for.

"That's not good," I drawled, seeing if she knew what I was. But she stood there in her little dress, perfuming profusely, unaware of her effect on me. My breathing quickened, and all the blood rushed down. I had to control myself, or else she'd wonder what the fuck was wrong with me.

Did she think she was human? Where the hell was her family? Why was she out here? I had so many questions. Questions I couldn't ask her.

"Are you going to arrest me?" she asked in a small voice,

eyelashes fluttering as she gazed up at me. Her face was pink, and she crossed her arms as if to stop her scent from filling the air. This omega was nervous as hell. I could sense her tension and nervousness as she stood there.

"What's your name?" I asked, pulling out a pen and paper as if this was official duty. This had suddenly turned personal to me.

"Tiana," she said. "I swear I won't do this again. I've never been to jail before."

"I'm Officer Grant, and since this is your first offense, this will be a misdemeanor," I said. "The car will be towed, though."

"Okay," she said, nodding her head shakily. "I guess we'll take a taxi then."

"Something that you should have thought to do from the beginning," I said roughly. She could have hurt herself. "I will give you both a ride home."

"Oh, that's very nice of you," she said. "But it's okay, we're good."

"I insist," I said, and she noticed the change in my tone. I realized I needed to lessen the alpha bark in my voice immediately, or else she'd know I wasn't an ordinary human guy.

Once they were both in the car, I drove to her friend's address that Tiana provided. This omega had bad choices in friends. I couldn't stand her talking and loudness as she blabbed on about her car being towed. She was pissed.

"Even though you're annoying as hell, you're hot," her friend said to me.

"Thanks," I said gruffly as Tiana laughed softly. The omega thought this was funny. I thought the friend was a nuisance that needed to be dropped off at home as soon as possible.

"Tiana, maybe he could be your boyfriend," she said. "Does he fit your requirements?"

"Lori, please," sighed Tiana, and I smiled while driving. It was her turn to feel uncomfortable by her friend's random remarks. I wanted to know all about this omega. *Did she even have a boyfriend? Did she live in isolation?*

After we dropped off her friend at her apartment, I started driving to where Tiana lived. She hesitated to give me her address but realized she didn't have a choice. Did her parents coach her into not telling anyone where she lived? If so, that was why I couldn't trace her.

"Do you live with family?" I asked in a conversational tone. If I could get her to trust me, she would open up.

"Yes, with my parents," she said slowly. "And I have a boyfriend too."

"So he lives with you too?" I asked, knowing full well she wasn't mated to anyone. It was impossible that she was mated. Especially the way she was perfuming in my car right now.

"I...uhh," she stumbled, realizing none of it made sense. "Yes, yes, he does."

"Tell me about him."

"He's umm, big and plays football," she said, her voice trailing off. As I stared at her in the rearview mirror, I admired how her cheeks turned pink and how she refused to look me in the eye. Maybe some part of her warned her that there was an alpha nearby.

I was the predator. And she was my prey.

When we reached her apartment, I parked the car in front of the building.

"I'd like to walk you inside. Is that alright?" I said to her as we both got out of the car.

She bit her lip.

"I don't need you to walk me inside," she protested. But I needed to see her living situation. I needed to know everything about her.

Before I took her.

"Just want to make sure you're safe," I said, and she nodded without a word. I followed her to the apartment building, watching her hands tremble as she unlocked the main glass door. We walked down a long narrow hallway that smelled of cigarettes and cats. Then she stopped in front of her door and tried to quietly unlock it, but the door flew open before she could stick the key in.

"You're late," said an older woman who looked similar to Tiana. She smiled politely when she saw me, but her face turned white, and I knew she knew what I was. An alpha were-wolf at her doorstep. "Did you get yourself into trouble being out so late?"

"Lori was drunk, so I drove her car," said Tiana, sounding exhausted. She sounded like she'd rather be anywhere else but here.

"Is she in trouble, officer?" asked the mother.

"No, since she has no past offenses," I reassured her. I didn't want her to be too harsh on this soft omega. I realized I needed to stop now before feelings grew on my end. I couldn't fall for this omega. "Have a good night, folks."

"Goodnight," said Tiana as we made eye contact. It was like electricity between us when we locked eyes, and her mother ushered her inside quickly to block her. Like a stunned man, I quickly pulled my phone out, dialing my packmate's number.

"Yo, yo," greeted Antonio.

"Tony, I found her," I said.

"God damn, after all these years?!"

"She must have been hiding or taking her omega heat suppressant pills," I said, trying to think of how this elusive omega survived for years without an alpha pack to protect her.

"It looks like our mission here on the human lands is done," said Tony. "It's sad because the humans love my guitar playing."

"You've gotten attached to human life," I said dryly. "Tell Wesley the good news. We'll meet up tomorrow and go through all her files. We have her name now."

"Sounds good, cop," said Tony. "I can't wait to go back home. I almost forgot what Howl's Edge looks like."

"Let's hope Tiana agrees to go with us. Or it'll be by force."

"Is that her name? Is she hot?"

"She's not for us, Tony," I drawled. Knowing I couldn't have her for myself bothered me, and I didn't know why. I barely knew her, for fuck's sake. "We were here for one mission- to get her home."

"Shit, calm down," said Tony.

"I want to see you and Wesley tomorrow at eleven a.m. sharp at the police department."

"You got it."

I hung up, stuffing my phone back in my pocket. I went around to the back of the building and shed my clothing. Then I shifted into my wolf form. Fur shot out from every part of my body, and my body lowered to the ground.

Long, sleek, and powerful.

Making my way around the building, I followed her scent. Lifting my snout in the air, I could smell a hint of her strawberry scent.

Her scent was soft yet elusive, and I felt myself responding to it on a deeper level. I haven't been around an omega wolf for more than twenty years. I've had human girlfriends now and then, but they were never long-term. At the age of thirty-nine, I was tired of the human ladies.

I tried to block my feral thoughts. But I couldn't control my thoughts. The smell of her scent was making my inner alpha go crazy. My alpha wolf wanted her underneath my body.

To rut her senseless. My wolf cock was throbbing as I bounded around the building, looking for her window.

I had to bring back the lost omega.

All I knew was that we had to bring an omega back. No other details of the mission were given to me when I was a teen. So, I decided to become a cop along with my pack. It was the only way we'd have more information on people.

And by god, it worked.

All my years of waiting around in this godforsaken land to finally go home and finish my mission was like a dream.

The dream of going back to Howl's Edge was close now.

I sniffed the dilapidated apartment building that said *Brenview Heights*. The building was painted green, half the paint peeled or chipped. The front door to the building was closed, and there was no way I could enter it now. Circling the building, I peered into every window. Lots of TVs were on, which was when people generally got home from work. I looked up, sensing her presence at one of the windows.

Tiana was on the first floor and peering out of the window.

My heart stopped beating momentarily as I gazed at her beauty. Her curly black hair was loose around her shoulders as she looked out, and her neck was flushed red. Then she pulled the curtain closed, accidentally leaving a gap open. I stayed there for a while, watching her as she plopped on her bed in her pajamas.

Then suddenly, she lifted her legs and spread them wide open with her pants still on.

I gasped in surprise. This little mama had a dirty side to her.

My wolf cock instantly hardened, watching her through the window. My breathing escalated as I watched her dip one finger hesitantly between her legs underneath her pajama bottoms. Like she wasn't sure of what she was doing.

I wanted to be there.

I wanted to be the one to make her cum. To dip my face between her juicy thighs. To lick her pussy until she screamed my name over and over.

I howled as I watched her try to pleasure herself, and I didn't give a fuck who heard me.

Three

TIANA

I was actually feeling aroused.

Never in my life did I think I'd ever feel like this. No man ever awakened these feelings inside of me. The feeling of warmth and the tingling between my legs was a lot, and I needed relief so badly. Feelings that I thought were dormant forever.

Ever since meeting the cop, it was like my body was in overdrive. My body craved him. I had no idea what to think. *Was it because he was good-looking?* But I've come across handsome guys before. So that didn't make sense.

It was like some weird ethereal force between us that I couldn't explain.

In my room, I closed my eyes and envisioned him as I rubbed myself. I was scared to touch myself in this way, but I needed relief. I slowly rubbed myself while still wearing my pajama bottoms. My pussy was throbbing and pulsing.

I needed Grant. I wanted him.

I wanted him to fill me up. I envisioned his tall, lean body on top of mine, humping and thrusting into me.

Just then, a long howl ripped through the air. *What the*

hell? I quickly sat up, bewildered. I walked to the window, about to peer through the curtains, when harsh knocking sounded on my bedroom door at that exact moment.

"Come in," I called out. My parents burst into the room.

"What was that?" asked my mom.

"It sounded like a mating howl," my dad whispered to her, even though I could clearly hear him.

"What the heck are you guys talking about?" I asked blithely, picking up my romance book from my nightstand. Sometimes, my father made weird remarks, which I often ignored. My mom began looking around my room as if in search of something.

"Where is it?!" she shouted.

"Where is what? You're freaking me out."

"The pills. The pills that I told you to take," she said.

"In the bathroom," I said.

"Show me," she said.

I slowly walked across the room and went to the bathroom in my room -grabbing the bottle. I felt like an entire kid all over again. *Why the fuck was I so scared?* I realized I had never stood up to my parents before, especially my mom.

I was always their little girl, and that made me angrier.

"Here it is," I said.

"Have you been taking it?" inquired my dad, looking at me like he knew what was up. I didn't want to lie. It was time I told them the truth.

"No," I said. "What the heck are they anyway?"

The smell from my body was overwhelming. Maybe someone had spilled a strawberry drink all over me. I needed to take a shower big time.

"Oh my god, no, no, no," my mom wailed, holding her face in her hands.

"What is it?" I asked. She was losing her damn mind over nothing.

I had to know what was going on once and for all. I sat on the edge of my bed, watching my dad comfort her, his arm around her.

"Tiana, it's time we explained something to you that we should've told you years ago," said my father.

My mom sat on the floor in front of me, tears running down her face.

"It might be hard to believe," my dad started. "But we are a family that has werewolf blood in our veins."

I shut my eyes tight for a second.

What in the actual hell? Was he serious right now? I took in a deep breath.

"Dad, you're pranking me right now," I said. "That's not even funny."

"We don't shift into werewolves anymore. Only the alphas still have the power to do that. Over the generations, our werewolf abilities have been diluted. I'm an alpha, and your mother is a beta," he explained.

I sat there stunned on the edge of my bed, not knowing what to think.

It was quiet for two minutes as my mind raced with all possibilities. Dad didn't look like he was joking. There was no sign of a smile like he usually did when he liked to prank me. His large black beard did not shake with unspoken laughter.

He was as serious as could be.

"So you can shift? I'm not buying this, Dad," I said. At first, I thought they were overprotective, and now they were delusional. How could I take them seriously now?

He rubbed his beard and sighed. "I haven't shifted since we came here to escape Howl's Edge with you as a baby."

"Is that the island you and Mom keep talking about?"

"Yes," he said. "When we left, we bought a whole bunch of heat suppressant pills for you."

"And what are those pills?" I asked, confused. Even

though none of this made sense, this was the most I was finally getting from them. An explanation, finally.

"To umm...suppress your emotions."

Scrunching my eyebrows, I looked at him like he had lost it.

"What are you talking about? Just say it clearly. I'm grown," I demanded.

"Those pills squashed your urges to date anyone, and it kept your scent hidden from any werewolves looking for you," said my mom.

Suddenly, everything fell into place. Ever since I stopped taking those pills, my feelings have grown stronger. My emotions were heightened, and I felt the urge to be with a man.

Anger began growing inside me at the horrible secret my parents kept from me.

Like I was a damn kid.

"Why did you give me the pill? Don't I deserve happiness too?" I asked, my voice breaking.

"Yes, baby," my mom said in a calmer voice. "I wanted to keep you safe because you were special."

"Special, how?"

"You're an omega. The rarest kind. The kind all male alphas fight over and would kill for," she explained. "I needed to take you away from all that. For your safety. We snuck on a supply boat here, unsure of what the future would hold."

"Why didn't you explain this to me years ago?"

"I'm sorry," said Mom. "But now you're in danger, and we need to move away from here. Start packing tonight. We need to leave immediately. The howl outside sounds like an alpha wolf."

"How about your jobs?" I asked.

"We only care about your safety."

"If you had told me this years ago, this wouldn't have

happened," I stood up and walked to the window, my arms crossed. I wasn't going to get up and leave the state because my parents said so.

My mom was losing her patience, "start packing, Tiana. We have to go before anyone tracks you down."

My parents left the room, closing the door behind them. As always, I was forced to do whatever they told me. I never had a voice.

How could they let me go around not knowing what I truly was? I couldn't believe them. Anger filled me as I stuffed my clothes in a small suitcase.

I wasn't going to go with my parents. I wasn't going to let them be burdened with me anymore.

Pulling out my phone, I texted Lori that I was coming over.

I was so done being under the control of my overprotective parents. It was time I lived my own life. If I couldn't feel passion or love for the rest of my life, what kind of life would that be? That wasn't fair to me.

After I frantically packed my essential stuff and everything I would need for the trip, I decided to write a letter:

Dear Mom & Dad,

I know you're probably freaking out about where I went. Don't worry, I'm going on a cruise trip for a week to think about things and will be back soon. So don't worry about moving because of me or quitting your job. I can take care of myself. Thank you for telling me about my true self, and it's time I explore what that means. I want to figure out myself and decide what I want. I'll be home soon!

Love you both,

Tiana

I laid the letter out in the middle of my bed, staring at it for a good moment. It sounded a little too cheerful. But in reality, I was conflicted and torn inside. I had never felt so alone in my life.

Was I doing the right thing? Inside, my feelings were in a frenzy. I knelt and cried on the edge of the bed. My tears soaked through the blanket.

I shuddered as I wept, scared of what the future held for me.

Four

GRANT

The next day, I sat in my office waiting for my packmates to arrive. I remembered Tiana's tears as I watched her through the window last night.

She was lonely, and I realized then that I should never have howled like that, getting her parents' attention.

It was reckless on my part.

Tiana's tears struck a chord inside me. I had to stop myself with all my power from breaking through the window and embracing her. I felt the loneliness in her heart. I could relate to that feeling.

I tapped my pen against the desk, leaning back against my chair. My office was small compared to the chief's, but I didn't care. I wasn't going to be here any longer, so I didn't give a fuck about my impending promotion. I would be rich soon once I turned this lost omega over.

The door opened, and Tony walked in, with Wesley following close behind.

"Hey, boss," said Tony, flicking his obnoxiously long black hair back.

"What took you forever?" I greeted curtly.

"I had a music performance to do. Being a cop isn't the only thing I do, man," drawled Tony, setting his blasted guitar on his lap. That guitar never left Tony's side. This guy was way too chill to be on this mission.

Wesley, on the other hand, was quieter. I wondered how he even joined my pack, but his keen insight was what I needed today. He nervously brushed his short blond hair back.

"Wesley, how are you?" I asked.

"I'm good. I'm excited to meet this Tiana of ours," he said.

"As I said, she's not ours," I said. "So what did we find out?"

"She's supposed to go on a cruise this Saturday," Wesley said. "You gave me her friend's address, and I sat outside the living room window last night listening to their plans."

"A cruise?!" I roared, slamming my fist on the desk. After all the years it took to find her, we couldn't lose sight of this omega.

"Why, what's wrong with that?" asked Wesley, his hands up.

"She can go into heat at any time! She's never gone into heat," I said, suddenly worried. After overhearing her conversation with her parents, she had no idea what an omega was and what it meant. She was in grave danger, especially since she wasn't taking her pills.

"Well then, we go on the cruise with her," said Tony.

"How the fuck do we invite ourselves onto a random cruise, genius?"

Wesley showed us his phone with the wedding invite open. " After digging around, I hacked into the registry and found the invite. It says they need security guards. We can call the number."

"Nice job," I said, impressed. Wesley's quick investigation skills were what I needed at this moment.

I grabbed my desk phone and quickly dialed the number on the wedding invitation.

"*Paradise Cruises*, how can I help you?"

"You have a flyer requesting security guards. I can assist with that, and so could two of my work buddies," I said, holding my breath.

"Okay, email us your credentials and experience. We'll be in touch."

I hung up, uncertain. But after they saw our years of experience being cops, we'd get approved in no time.

"Start packing for the trip, men," I said. "We'll figure out how to bring her to Howl's Edge once we're on that ship with her."

"Woo! Our lives are finally getting interesting," said Tony, playing a tune on the guitar. "I wonder if she's beautiful."

"All omegas are stunning," said Wesley.

I rolled my eyes as the two men conversed about the cruise trip and meeting an omega. When we first moved here, they were young in their early teens, and they had no experience with omegas. I was the oldest of the pack, so naturally, they looked to me as the leader.

I just hoped they had a little more self-control than me. They had no idea how alluring an omega's scent was, and from what I observed of Tiana, her scent was dimmed, but it was there.

Because the next time I saw her, I didn't know how I'd keep my hands to myself.

Five

TIANA

"**S**pread," ordered Grant. He knelt in front of me, his jaw tense.

My legs spread open on the bed. As if there was an invisible force separating them against my will.

"Is this good?" I asked.

"Good girl," said Grant. "Men, come and take a peek at our omega."

Three men I had never seen before walked into the bedroom, their eyes glued to my sex. I writhed under their gazes, immensely turned on.

"Her pussy is dripping," said the man with a ponytail.

"Please touch me," I begged, spreading my legs wider, my breathing quickening and my pulse pounding.

Suddenly, I woke up with a gasp.

I sat up on the couch, my hand clutching my chest in shock. My panties were damp as hell. What the hell was that dream about? Why was I dreaming of having sex? I just met the cop last night, and I was having such explicit dreams.

"What's wrong?" asked Lori carrying a bowl of frosted flakes and making her way over to the couch. I was at Lori's apartment after taking a taxi to her house last night and being fed up with my parents.

I still didn't believe what my parents said and didn't want to think about what they said. There was no way in hell I was going to take the pills again. They were delusional and needed to be checked. They'd fill me up with drugs and more shit I didn't need. I looked at my phone, seeing a bunch of missed calls from Mom.

I did a little research on the Internet about alphas, and it sent me into a rabbit hole of knotting and how they liked to dominate their omega. So I slept aroused as hell.

It was going to be hard to trust them again.

"I had the most stupid nightmare," I sighed, stretching. My heart was still racing from the naughty dream, but I was starting to calm down a little.

"Share the dream," she said, eating her cereal and watching me with concern in her wide eyes like nothing had happened with her car last night.

"I dreamt I was about to have sex with four guys. Like all at once," I said.

Saying it out loud made it sound so ridiculous.

"Whoa, girl, it looks like someone is sex-starved 'round here," laughed Lori, droplets of milk flying from her mouth. "I wouldn't mind a couple of guys myself."

"It was just…bizarre," I said, shaking my head. "Glad the cruise is today."

"Yeah, you've been too stressed about classes and family," said Lori. "Pack your best shit. We gotta look nice and attract some guys."

"Do you remember what happened last night?" I asked, watching her face.

"It was so vague," she answered. "I barely remember a thing. I think you got pulled over, and then I ended up at home."

"Your car is towed," I said. "We can't be partying like that again, Lori."

"Shit, I completely forgot," said Lori. "That sucks so bad. I'm sorry for putting you in that position to drive."

"I forgive you," I said.

"We'll worry about the car when we return from vacation."

"I guess," I laughed, removing the plaid printed sheet from my lap and going to the bathroom.

After brushing, showering, and getting dressed in a red sundress, I felt ready to go. I already packed most of my things last night at my parent's place.

I wore a black cardigan over my dress. I stared at Lori's vanity mirror, applying my mascara. I had curled my shoulder-length black hair and had to keep brushing off the little tendrils of curls covering my eyes.

I patted my hair down, happy with how I looked.

"Do you have extra sunglasses?" I asked Lori, who was scrambling to find something to wear.

"Yep, in the top drawer of the vanity," she called from the closet.

Putting on the sunglasses, I felt sexy as I twirled in front of the mirror. I wanted to meet some guys on purpose this time. Maybe it would work since I was fixed now with all my emotions. Wet dreams and all.

I unzipped my suitcase, making sure everything I needed was in there.

"I'm ready to go," I said. "We're going to be so late, Lori. The cruise leaves in an hour, and it will take us time to get there."

"I know," she sighed, sinking against her few outfits in the closet. "I have literally nothing to wear."

Maybe a vacation to the Bahamas is just what I needed to let loose.

AFTER THE CHAOTIC morning with Lori trying to find an outfit, we walked along the boarding deck to the cruise ship.

It was a sunny morning, and the slight chill in the wind made me shiver. I wrapped my cardigan tighter around me. We stood in line as everyone's bags were checked at the front by security guards.

"That's my cousin," said Lori, pointing her out.

"She doesn't look too happy," I said, looking at the bride wearing a thin white dress. She had curly blond hair and red lipstick. She was in the front of the line, clutching her fiance's hand and tapping his arm constantly. He looked like he couldn't be bothered to talk.

"Yep, the one and only," said Lori. "Not looking forward to greeting her." Lori could be right. Her cousin looked like the definition of a bridezilla.

As we reached the front, one of the security guys looked up, tipping his hat up.

When I saw who it was, I froze.

It was Grant. Out of *all* freaking people.

I turned around, ready to run away, but Lori pulled my arm.

"What are you doing?" she hissed at me. Of course she didn't recognize the cop from last night. She was too out of it.

I noticed the line behind us. They were looking annoyed.

Shit. I didn't have a choice. Either go back to my parents or go on a cruise with some hot cop who knew where I lived and knew I crashed a stop sign.

I took a deep breath and turned back to face Grant.

"We need to pat you down for any weapons," he said in his gravelly voice. His voice sent a tingle down my spine, and I almost forgot the effect it had on me. It disarmed me completely as I stood there waiting for his touch. Looking forward to his hand running all over my body.

I stood with my arms out to the side.

Grant waved over the other security guard to take care of Lori, and then he stood in front of me. He wore a white uniform with a medallion on the front. The gun at his side stood out, turning me on even more for some freaky reason.

When his brown hands touched my arms, my skin heated despite the cold. He rubbed my arms and slowly went down my sides, deliberately taking his time in my chest area. My breathing intensified as his hands rested against my hips momentarily, and then he released me.

"You're good," he said softly, looking at me with hooded eyes.

Flushed, I quickly walked onto the deck, my suitcase flopping behind me as I dragged it. Kids and families assembled on the large deck as workers directed them where to go. I leaned against the railing, waiting for Lori to get her bags checked.

I had no idea how Grant ended up on the ship with us and what he was doing here. Could it be a total coincidence?

"That was interesting," said Lori. "Two hot as fuck security guys. We're going to have fun."

For some reason, a stab of jealousy went through me when she noticed Grant. I bit my lip at how ridiculous I was being. I had no right to be possessive of anyone.

"Let's figure out where our rooms are," I said finally.

I unpacked my suitcase on my bed. I was sharing a room with Lori. She was already sprawled out on her bed. Her items were scattered all over the place.

"I'm starving," she said, holding her stomach.

"Didn't you just eat cereal before we got here?" I asked,

my mind distracted as I thought about Grant's hands patting me down.

"Well, it's lunchtime now," she said, sitting up. She was wearing a purple crop top with purple leggings. She hated dressing up, and I tried to convince her to dress a little fancier, but she said she'd only do that on the actual wedding day, which was tomorrow.

"I don't want to go up there right now," I said, my stomach growling. I hadn't had breakfast since I was nervous about leaving my family for so long. Now, I was a bit nervous that Grant was on the ship with us.

It was better hiding away here. I sat on the bed, feeling slightly dizzy and an incessant throbbing between my legs. I rubbed my warm forehead, hoping I wasn't getting sick.

"Why not?"

"I'm just not feeling so good right now."

"Alright, I'll see you when you decide to come up."

I nodded, closing my eyes.

"My cousin put us all the way in the back," huffed Lori, looking around the room. "Typical. It's like I don't matter or something."

At least we were here, and I wanted to say. But I didn't want to piss her off or act like I was on her cousin's side. When Lori was hungry, there was no stopping her anger.

I finished unpacking and sat on the bed, clutching my belly. I felt minor cramps down there, but nothing too major. Twinges of arousal kept going through me, and my privates were clenching.

That's it. I had to take care of this once and for all.

I walked into the tiny bathroom in our room and closed the door behind me. I had never masturbated before, so I was scared of what to expect. But I needed some relief and quick. The pills really messed with me. Suppressing me my entire life.

I reached under my dress and lightly traced my underwear

with my finger. It was like I had to get acquainted with myself first. Bolts of arousal strummed through my body as I rubbed outside my underwear, getting wetter. My breathing quickened, and I was throbbing now.

Moving my panties to the side, I touched a finger to my clitoris. I cried out as I basked in the brand-new sensation.

Six

GRANT

"Is she the omega?" asked Tony, coming up to me, his face flushed red. His long black hair flew wildly around his face from the wind. "I could smell her scent. My god."

"She is," I said gruffly. "Someone needs to be around her at all times. She's proven to be irresponsible."

"How can you resist her scent?" said Wesley. "We need an omega in our pack."

"It doesn't matter. We are not to mate her," I said.

"Even if she goes into heat?" asked Tony.

I didn't have an answer for him. That would be the worst case scenario. Something I wasn't prepared for.

Suddenly, I heard a small whimper coming from below deck. Only an omega would make that sound. My heart pounding, I knew we could be in trouble if she was in heat at this very second.

"Wesley and Tony, take care of the rest of the guests coming on board," I barked. "I need to check on something."

They looked at me, bewildered, as I rushed out of there. I went down the steps, my body too tall to fit through, but I managed to squeeze down into the lower deck. My alpha senses were on alert as I followed Tiana's harsh breathing down the hall.

Bursting into her room, I couldn't see her anywhere. Then I realized she was in the bathroom.

I was being ridiculous. She was probably peeing in there. I put my ear to the door and heard her cry out again. I knocked on the door, and immediately the sounds stopped. Twisting the doorknob open, I saw her standing there with her hand between her legs underneath her dress.

She looked up at me, her eyes wide and guilty. She looked like she was in the middle of touching herself. Her back was flush against the wall, her face pink.

And by god, that was the hottest thing I had ever witnessed.

My balls clenched, and my dick immediately hardened upon gazing at her in her vulnerable state.

"Get out," she said, quickly straightening her dress and covering herself. But her voice had wavered, and she looked at me uncertainly.

"Have you ever touched yourself before?" I asked, walking inside and shutting the door behind me.

The little bathroom was small and cramped. My body mere inches away from hers. I felt like a hulking monster towering over her petite body.

Her omega scent was strong right now while she was aroused. The thick, heavy strawberry smell in the air made me heady with desire. I hadn't been around an omega for years since I was trapped in the human lands looking for her.

My hands itched to cup those soft boobs and bury my cock inside her hot pussy.

"This is wrong. You're a cop," she said, uncertain as she stood before me. "You can't ask me these things."

"I know what you are," I said. "What you truly are."

Her eyebrows shot up in surprise.

"Then what am I?" she asked.

"An omega," I said. "And it's normal for you to feel this way. I will explain later after I take care of you. Have you ever touched yourself before?"

"No," she whimpered, looking down. She looked upset. "I can't orgasm. I don't know how."

She was in a state of arousal, and she needed release but didn't know how to. I remembered how hesitant she was touching herself in her bedroom. I quickly turned to the sink and washed my hands. Then I faced her.

"Turn around," I commanded.

"Why?" she asked, about to turn but stopped with uncertainty.

"Let me help you," I said. "I will touch your pussy and make you cum. Do you want that, Tiana?"

She bit her lower lip as her face flushed. Then she turned around, her back facing me.

"Yes," she said quietly.

I sensed her need. Her desperation for release.

Her butt looked magnificent, jutting out from her little sundress. Taunting me.

I pressed up against her, breathing in her scent at her neck. My cock pressed in between her ass cheeks, nestling in the middle. She gasped as I pressed my mouth against her neck, purring into her. My vibrations calmed her tense body as I felt her sink into me. I slowly reached around and rubbed her belly softly, bringing my hand further down.

Lifting her dress from the front, I pressed my pointer finger around her lacy panties. It was drenched from her prior efforts. Fuck, I lifted my finger to my nose, smelling her scent. Her scent was powerful and potent.

Her musky fruity odor sent my body into overdrive, my dick rock hard.

"What are you doing?" she inquired, looking into the mirror. Her eyes were round and wide as she watched me smell my finger with her juices all over it. I licked my finger.

"Tasting you," I said. "Take off your panties and give them to me."

I could feel her butt jiggle against my cock as she bent down, removing her underwear. Then she looked away from the mirror as she handed it to me. The red lace panties had a dark, wet stain on the seat of it.

"Is this necessary?" she asked, sounding embarrassed.

"You wet your panties," I growled, sniffing the dark stain. I inhaled her scent and the slight smell of strawberry. She smelled amazing, and I felt like I would lose my goddamn fucking mind if I didn't get to fuck her immediately. "Open your legs. Now."

I dropped the panties next to the toilet and patted her thighs to prod her open. I felt her legs trembling.

"I'm sorry," she said. "I'm just so nervous. I've never had someone touch me there before."

I purred in her ear again until she willingly let her legs open.

I used my feet to spread her legs apart wider. Then I reached around and felt her soaking wet pussy. She was wet and needy. Her slick soaked my fingers as I rubbed her folds and all around, feeling her pussy. I felt her shiver in response to my touch, and she started to hump my finger. I pressed against her swollen clit, rubbing in circles.

"Do you want me to rub faster and harder?" I asked her.

"Yes," she said with a note of urgency.

"Say yes, alpha," I commanded while lightly rubbing her clit. She suddenly froze.

"Are you an alpha?"

"Mhm," I said, annoyed that I had given away my cover.

Either way, she would know sooner or later. "Don't focus on that right now. I want you to focus on your pleasure."

"Yes, alpha." She tried to hump my finger, but I kept it elusive.

"Yes, what?"

"Yes, alpha, please rub my pussy faster and harder," she finally pleaded.

Pressing my thumb against her clit, I rubbed up and down. Adding pressure. Faster and faster. Tiana shook and trembled in my arms. Her soft body pressed against my hard one, and I reveled in it. The crown of my cock leaked as I watched her in her first orgasm. We were both staring in the mirror, her pink pussy on display as I fingered her.

"Cum for me, sweetheart."

She yelled out, her thighs trembling and shaking. Then, her lush body collapsed against me as she took fast, shallow breaths. Her large breasts heaved up and down. My hard cock was still pressed between her ass.

I rubbed her juices between my fingers, bringing them to my mouth.

"I want a taste of your sweet slick," I sighed, licking my fingers. Then I placed my two fingers in her mouth, and she hesitantly sucked. "Good girl."

"Oh, this is so embarrassing," said Tiana, covering her face. I immediately spun her around to face me, pulling her hands away from her beautiful face. Her face was flushed with a tinge of red.

"Don't be embarrassed. It's natural to feel urges, and you're going to get them all the time."

"Okay," she said. "It's just a little weird that you had to help me."

"It's not weird, don't worry," I said.

"Why are you here? On the ship?"

She was a sharp one and got right to it. I touched her forehead with the back of my palm. She was a little warm, and I worried she could be in pre-heat.

"I'm a security guy. Also, you shouldn't have stopped the pills your parents gave you," I said, growing concerned. She looked like she was going to go into heat soon. And it had better not be on this ship.

"Wait, how do you know about that?" She pulled away, looking shocked.

"I was the wolf howling outside your room," I said. "You're an omega, and I'm an alpha wolf. That's why your body naturally wants to be around me."

"I can't believe this. I knew I felt something different with you," she said, shaking her head. "You're an actual werewolf?"

"Yes," I said. "You were on the pill for too damn long, suppressing your omega side. But now you're in danger of going into heat."

"What? How is being horny dangerous?"

"Just promise me that if you start hurting, you'll let me know," I said.

"Okay," she answered after some hesitation. Someone started knocking on the bathroom door.

"I'll see you around," I said, turning away from her soft brown eyes before I fucked her senseless. I opened the door. Her friend with that ridiculous purple outfit walked into the room, her eyes wide as she looked between Tiana and me.

She was speechless.

I chuckled as I left.

Seven

TIANA

"Oh my, what just happened?" asked Lori with a wink.

"Nothing," I said quickly, sinking into my bed and wondering that myself. *Did it really happen? Did Grant just finger me?!* A complete and total stranger.

I buried my face in the pillow, mortified as hell. Then I turned to face her.

"You are so lying. Tell me," Lori asked eagerly, plopping on her bed cross-legged. I could see cookie crumbs on the knees of her purple leggings. "Tiana, if you don't tell me...I swear to God."

I was tongue-tied. I didn't know what to tell her exactly. I couldn't tell her the truth without revealing what I was. That I was some kind of mysterious omega werewolf.

She would run screaming.

"I...we kissed," I lied.

"Oh my," she said, staring at me in fascination. "I'm so happy for you! And he's hot as fuck on top of that."

"Um, thanks," I laughed softly. I still couldn't process what had happened. Why did I allow that to happen? How did I let my body take control like that? To open myself to him so easily shocked me senseless. But I felt so relaxed for the first time in days after my first orgasm.

"Now you have a date for tomorrow's wedding ceremony," said Lori. "I talked with the hot captain while I ate lunch upstairs."

"That's good," I said, lost in my hazy thoughts.

"Look at us finally getting out of our shells," she said. "So what's your man like?"

"He's not my man," I protested. "But I agree he's hot. I don't know if he thinks this is serious or just a little fling."

"Just have fun on the trip," said Lori. "No expectations. Flirt and have fun. That's what I'm doing."

"What are you wearing for the wedding tomorrow?"

"I don't know," said Lori, and I chuckled.

We laughed and talked about her cousin. The wedding. And her cousin again, and how much Lori disliked her. I munched on potato chips since I was starting to feel a little sick from the ship rocking on the waters.

"I think I should call my mom," I said, throwing the empty bag of chips into the bin. I looked out the little window above us, seeing the twinkling stars. I felt like I missed my parents a little, and they were probably freaking out since I had never spent the night away from home.

"Maybe you should," said Lori. "I cut my mom off years ago, but I don't want that to happen to you."

"Alright then," I said, grabbing my phone.

I dialed my mom's number, my heart pounding.

"Please leave a message after the tone," greeted the voicemail.

"Hey, Mom," I said. "I'm on the cruise now, and I just wanted to say that I'm safe. Okay, bye."

I hung up. I had never defied my parents like this—well, not to this extreme. I wondered for a second if my mom ignored the call on purpose, but I dismissed the negative thoughts. I didn't want to feel down right now after my high with Grant.

"At least you called," said Lori. "No need for you to feel guilty anymore, knowing you."

"Haha, very funny," I said, grabbing a towel and heading to the bathroom.

I needed to shower and get clean. I felt guilty in other ways. Letting a man touch me for the first time was one of those.

I scrubbed my body with the white loofah, covering my body with bubbly soap. I was aching again between my legs as the loofah brushed over my skin. My skin was warm down there and sensitive to any touch. I was a horny mess right now. Grant had relieved some of it, but I could feel an emptiness that needed to be filled.

Like a hollow feeling in my belly.

I quickly rinsed all the soap off, trying to think of other things instead. He said he was an alpha and that I was naturally inclined to him. It seemed a little weird, but it had me once again turned on at the thought. It felt nice to have someone understand me, and I didn't feel so alone in my struggle to figure out what I was. I was determined to find out more about what I was and where our people truly came from.

AFTER MY SHOWER, I decided to stroll above deck and enjoy this vacation a little bit. I wasn't prepared for the crisp breeze outside as I only wore a pink tank top and shorts. Probably not the wisest choice of clothes.

I had left Lori asleep in the cabin. The stars littered the night sky, and the dark waves of the ocean sparkled. Exploring the deck of the ship, I admired wedding decorations and the grand pillars erected in every corner. There were still quite a few people out at night having a good time. I held onto the railing as I looked out at the peaceful waters. I gazed into the oblivion of the water, imagining sharks swimming underneath us.

"Enjoying the view?" asked a voice from my left.

Startled, I turned my head and saw Grant. He was also leaning against the railing, but his eyes were on me.

"You scared me," I said softly.

"Are you feeling alright?" he asked, his attention completely zeroed in on me. Every time I was in his presence, the energy was super intense. It was never light.

"I'm fine," I said. "Are you enjoying the trip?"

"Apart from breaking up fights and dealing with crazy people- everything's dandy," he joked, and I smiled. "How are you enjoying your trip so far?"

"Well, it just started," I said, turning my attention back to the water. The ship suddenly rocked, and I stumbled. His arm snaked around my waist, holding me snugly against his warm body. "You're warm."

"Alphas have a higher body temperature," he explained against my ear as he held me. Feeling his hard planes of muscles behind me caused warmth to spiral through my belly again. I clenched my thighs at the sudden onset of arousal again.

"Oh."

"I shouldn't be this close to you," he said, releasing me. "You should go to your room."

Confused, I scrunched my eyebrows. Why was he saying this? He was acting like he wanted me a minute ago.

"Why are you telling me what to do?"

"I'm sorry," he sighed, letting out a long breath. "It's just best for the both of us."

"Uhh, I guess I'll see you tomorrow then?"

"Have a good night, Tiana," he said, his nostrils flared and his body tense.

"You too."

As I lay in bed that night, memories of Grant's large fingers strumming my clit had me wriggling and turning several times. The room was dark, and Lori was snoring full throttle, her arms hanging off the edge of her bed.

My breathing quickened, and my finger slipped underneath my panties.

I closed my eyes, trying to replicate what Grant did to me. I moved my finger in circles between my legs, teasing myself. The arousal in my abdomen grew worse, and then I quickly stopped. I didn't want to struggle with masturbation while my friend was in the room.

I closed my eyes, frustrated and aroused.

***

THE NEXT DAY was dark and gloomy for the wedding ceremony.

I sat in the back row with Lori and an empty seat to my right. We were out on the deck, rows of chairs lined up for the guests and a beautiful arch in front of us. Everything was decorated in blush pink and white. Little flamingos decorated the arch with white flowers. The chairs had large white silk bows tied in the back. Everyone was chattering and talking loudly as we waited for the ceremony to start.

Everything was beautiful except for the dark clouds above us. It looked like it was going to rain.

I noticed Grant standing on the corner of the deck in uniform, his eyes trained on me. And there was something else in his look. Like he was thinking of yesterday's events in the bathroom.

My breathing quickened as I looked away, my face hot.

"Look, this guy messaged me," said Lori excitedly, shoving her phone in my face. She was messaging someone all day, and I wondered who it was but knew she'd eventually tell me.

"He's cute," I said. His face was youthful and round, with an innocent expression on his face. "How old is he?"

"You don't want to know."

"Go on," I said.

"Fine, he's nineteen."

"He's kind of young for you," I said.

"Come on. I'm twenty-five," she said. "But he turns me on."

"I'm excited for you," I said. "But how about your poor captain?"

I looked over at the captain steering the wheel. He kept glancing over at Lori.

"He'll survive," she said, laughing and looking at the captain. When she saw him staring at her, I could see her cheeks visibly turning pink.

"Someone's blushing," I teased.

"May I sit here?" said a male voice next to me. I looked to my right and saw a tall man with long black hair tied into a ponytail. He had dark eyes and wore black clothes with chains on his shirt.

He was medium-height and built of muscle.

"Sure," I said, already starting to warm down there. My body was going haywire without the pills.

Oh, my goodness.

Was I doomed to get horny every time a dude looked my way now? I straightened my emerald green dress over my knees. It was a low-cut dress that showed off my shoulders and cleavage. I even put on quite a bit of makeup while Grant was in my mind.

Finally, the people quieted down, and the music started.

I watched as the groom and his groomsmen walked to the

front, standing next to the officiant in blue. I was hyper-aware of the nicely built man sitting quietly next to me. I looked back at Grant and saw him talking with another security officer with lake-blue eyes and caramel-colored hair. His face was clean-shaven, and he looked serious as he spoke with Grant. I wondered what they were talking about.

"Makes you wish you were getting married, huh?" commented the guy next to me.

"Oh?" I said, tearing my gaze away from Grant and his friend. I looked back at the ceremony. The bride and the groom were kissing now. "Sort of."

"What do you mean by 'sort of?'" asked the stranger next to me. I could hear the curiosity in his voice.

Wait, why the heck was he talking to me? I looked up at him, noticing his brown eyes had flecks of silver. I couldn't look away from his gaze. Something deep inside me stirred, wanting to claw at him. To bring him to me and inside of me.

He was a werewolf. I instinctively just knew from one glance. His alpha gaze seemed to pull me in and mesmerize my senses. How was I meeting these guys all of a sudden?

A spark shot between us, igniting my wonder and lust.

"The thought of marriage scares me. To be stuck with only one man for the rest of my life," I said.

His mouth turned up in a knowing smile.

"You have a point there," he said, sticking out his hand. "My name's Antonio, but you can call me Tony."

I couldn't ask him if he was a werewolf. Lori was right next to me. I wanted to ask to confirm I wasn't crazy, even though I knew one hundred percent that he was one.

"I'm Tiana," I said, shaking his hand.

"You're hot as fuck," he said right out.

"Oh, stop," I giggled. Inside, I grew shocked at myself for my behavior. *Why the fuck was I acting like a teen with a crush?*

"For real, though," he said insistently, pulling my hand in his. His hand was warm and large over mine, encasing it. We locked gazes, and I immediately thought of kissing him.

"It's time to dance now," said Lori loudly, breaking up my instant connection with this man. Annoyed, I gave her the side eye, and she smiled evilly.

"Dance with me?" asked Tony as we stood up from our chairs.

"Sure," I said.

We walked to the main dance area inside the glass doors. The music was blasting, and people were already drinking and getting down on the floor. I wanted to stand next to the railing to look at the beautiful ocean, but I wanted to get close to Tony. To feel his masculine body against mine.

He took my hand in his and gently led me to the dance floor.

When he pulled me towards him, I gasped. I wasn't prepared to feel the hardness of his chest against mine. I twirled and danced with this complete stranger. He was a pretty good dancer as he spun me around.

"Oh, I'm dizzy," I gasped, holding onto his strong forearm.

"You need more vitamins. Omegas need them," he whispered in my ear. My heart leaped in my chest, and I stopped breathing for a moment. He was admitting he knew what I was.

"How do you know?" I asked, surprised.

"I'm in Grant's pack. You've met him," he nodded towards Grant, who was overseeing the dance with his hawkish eyes. "We're the Frostcrown Pack."

"Oh," I said. "I'm sorry. I'm so new to this...werewolf stuff."

"Don't worry about it," he said.

"Why are you guys here on this ship?" I asked. "Or was it all coincidence?"

"Not a coincidence," he said. "When Grant met you, he wanted to find out everything about you, so naturally, we're here. Alphas are attracted to omegas. And we need an omega in our pack."

He looked unsure of himself as if he had said too much.

"I'm not going to say anything to Grant," I tried to reassure him, but my mind was racing with what he said. *Was Grant going to try and bring me into the pack? What was he going to do?*

He pulled me close when a slow song began, and I leaned against his chest. I could feel the heat emanating from his chest.

"Tiana," he began, and I lifted my head off his chest to look at him. I felt super comfortable with him.

"Yes?"

"Don't," he said.

Alarm bells rang in my head. "Don't what?"

"Don't get too attached or anything...we might not be for you."

Well, excuse me.

"I'm not getting attached. What the hell are you talking about?" I said defiantly, pulling my hands out of his grasp. "I just met you."

"What's going on here?" Grant demanded.

Eight

GRANT

"Grant, man, what's your problem?" demanded Tony. I knew he was pissed at me for interrupting his first dance with the omega.

Tiana's eyes flicked back and forth between us.

"I'm leaving," said Tiana. "I don't need this drama in my life right now."

I watched as she stalked away angrily from us.

"Why the fuck are you dancing with her?" I asked. "Wesley is over there doing his job. Why can't you follow orders?"

"It was just a dance," sighed Tony, looking up at the sky in exasperation. "You can't expect us alphas to ignore an omega on the ship with us. I was curious about her, that's all."

"I saw how she got comfortable with you. We can't allow her to get attached to us," I said in a low growl.

"You're fighting it. You want her," accused Tony, looking straight into my face.

My jaw clenched in anger. I wanted to punch him. But he was right.

A million percent right.

I looked back at her, seeing her mingle with her blond friend and the captain. The wind made her hair and dress fly around wildly. She looked so innocent and vulnerable. But my heart couldn't go there.

She was for another pack.

"We made a deal with the Lustfur pack," I said. "It needs to be done, and we'll bring her to them. I called Sam, and he'll be here tonight with his boat."

"So tonight we take her with us," said Tony, his eyes downcast. "I don't like this one bit."

I swallowed hard, my heart beating painfully slow. I didn't like it either. My inner alpha was growling in rage at the thought of handing her off to another pack. Especially to the Lustfur Pack. Any other pack was better.

"When she's mated with them and happily bonded, we'll forget about her. I assure you, Tony," I said, but I was comforting myself more with the thought.

"What if she's unhappy with them and wants to mate with us instead?"

"That's not happening unless you want to lose everything we're about to get," I reminded him. There was no way I would return to the poverty lifestyle I grew up with. I grew up as an orphan, thrown out into the streets as a pup.

The Lustfur Pack offered property and land in exchange for the stolen omega. When her parents left the island, it was rumored that they had a baby girl who had the mark of an omega. It was the first time in the history of Howl's Edge that parents had left the island. And the most powerful pack, the Lustfur pack, was not too happy about that. Even parents couldn't just take an omega out of Howl's Edge and get away with it. So, instead of her parents getting punished, we were doing Tiana a favor.

I had signed up to find the stolen omega, and it was going to be me who won the riches.

We looked over at her, and I saw her chatting with Wesley. She somehow found her way to another alpha.

"Ha, looks like she just can't help it," laughed Tony as we watched her flirt with Wesley.

"No, no, no, what the hell," I muttered, making my way over to them. Wesley looked surprised with those blue eyes of his as he saw me. Tiana didn't retreat like the last time. Instead, she turned to face me, fire in her eyes.

"What are you doing here?" she asked me, seething. "Is he your boyfriend, too?"

"No," I growled. I could see Tony's body shaking with laughter. Damn him.

"Then what's your problem with me? You had no issues breaking into the bathroom yesterday," she said, her eyes narrowed.

"Whoa," said Wesley, his eyebrows raised. "You did what, Grant?"

"Grant, you didn't tell us this," said Tony gleefully.

I took a deep breath to calm down. They were testing me.

"No, I didn't," I said calmly. "I might have been a little too strict on you all. Let's have lunch together since you're all dying to get to know each other."

"That sounds nice," said the little minx. Her nose was in the air, and she wasn't backing down. I never saw this side of her, and I was surprised. Her omega instincts wanted to be around alpha males, and I knew she couldn't help it, not knowing what she wanted from us. She needed a knot when she went into full heat. Several alpha knots inside her, actually. I knew exactly what she needed, but we couldn't touch her. Mating her wasn't on the table.

As she walked by me, her strawberry scent trailed behind her, putting my senses on alert.

I thought this would be easy, but I was starting to realize this would be a lot harder than I thought.

Nine

TIANA

Grant was being such a jerk. I didn't get what his problem was. He touched me, and now he's acting like nothing happened. *Was he jealous of his pack?* That had to be it.

"Let's sit here," said Wesley, pointing to a table next to the ship's edge. It had a good view of the ocean.

"It's perfect," I said, sitting at the round table covered in white cloth. Wesley and Tony sat on either side of me. Grant sat across from us, scowling. I was still upset with Tony for how he talked to me earlier, but I wasn't going to make a big deal about it now.

"Looks like it's about to rain," observed Tony.

"Yeah, it's pretty dark," I agreed, a little worried. The ship was bumpy, and the water was choppy. The sky was dark and covered with ominous clouds. It wasn't a great week for a cruise vacation. And I didn't trust the ship itself since I could hear every creak and groan. However, Lori did mention that her cousin was cheap, so I was worried about this old ship.

The waiter came to take our orders, and I noticed the bride and groom were taking pictures with their family. I felt terrible for Lori as she was dragged into it. She hated taking pictures, and I could see it on her face.

I looked back at the group of men I was sitting with. I had grown unsure of myself and remembered how miserable I was a few days ago being lonely.

I was drawn to them, and I didn't understand why. I felt like I belonged to them. I rubbed my hot forehead with my hand, wondering what the heck was going on with me.

This wasn't me. Or maybe it was the real me without the pills.

"Is everything alright?" Tony asked, touching my arm. His touch sent electricity shooting through my body and between my legs. If only he knew the havoc his touch was having on my body.

On my other side, Wesley's body heat was close to mine, which also had an effect. Grant's gaze on me was intense. I was surrounded by all kinds of masculine energy right now.

More than I've ever had before in years. Scratch that...*my life*.

"Yes," I lied. But my face was hot, and I was aching down there. I couldn't explain it. The nearness of their bodies was making my hormones go haywire again. I wanted Grant to do what he did to me yesterday.

"I don't think she's okay," observed Grant, staring at me from across the table. "She's about to go into heat."

I squirmed in my chair. His studying look was too invasive. Too intimate.

"I think so, too," said Tony, also staring into my face.

"Have you been feeling weird lately?" asked Wesley.

"I'm okay," I said so they wouldn't keep staring at me. The waiter brought my chicken salad. Even though I ached, I was starving. I couldn't remember the last time I ate. The chicken was so soft and delicious.

"Do you like Seattle?" asked Tony.

"I do," I said. "I miss my family, but they pissed me off after not telling me what I was for my entire life. I never knew about being an omega or anything like that."

I noticed a look pass between Tony and Grant. I shrugged and dug into the boiled egg in the salad. I was way too hungry to care about the ominous look.

"How would you feel if you never saw your home again?" asked Grant.

"What kind of question is that?" I asked, wondering if this was the official invite to their pack that Tony was talking about. "You guys are being weird."

I sipped the cold lemonade, and it was so delicious. I sat back in my chair, full and satisfied. But definitely not satisfied down there. A feeling of emptiness permeated through my body, causing my hand to tremble around the cold glass.

"Just wondering," said Tony.

"So what's a bunch of werewolves doing on a cruise ship?" I asked. We were talking about werewolves like it was nothing at all. Maybe I was starting to believe it.

"Just doing security work," said Wesley, panicked as he looked down at his uniform.

"I see," I said.

Suddenly, my abdomen started to hurt, and I held my stomach in pain.

"You okay?" Tony asked yet again.

"I'll be back," I whispered, my teeth clenching in pain as I ran out of there. I quickly shoved my way through the people, making my way downstairs and into the tiny hallway. Each step hurt as I walked to my room at the end of the long hallway.

I stepped inside the room and shut the door.

I felt something seeping between my legs, so I ran to the bathroom. Breathing hard, I sat on the toilet, nothing coming out. I was extremely wet. My underwear had clear white fluid that I'd never seen before.

I left the bathroom and lay on my bed, clutching my stomach. I've never had a period, but I've heard about girls having them and how painful it was. But there was no blood. I felt my womb clenching and more moisture gathering below.

I felt like I was physically empty inside the more aroused I became. The feeling wasn't pleasant at all.

I needed something inside me. To fill me up.

The pain grew more intense as I lay on the bed, holding my stomach. It felt like my body was squeezing in and spasming.

There was knocking on the door. Three firm knocks.

"Who is it?" I asked, my voice breathless as I rolled in pain, my head pressed against the limp white pillow drenched in sweat.

The door opened, and to my surprise, I saw Grant, Tony, and Wesley standing at the entrance. They quickly made their way inside, locking the door with a loud audible click.

Grant quickly came to my side, kneeling on the side of the bed.

"What are you feeling right now?" he asked me, gently pushing my hair away from my face.

"Squeezing and lots of wetness down there," I gasped as another sharp contraction wracked through my body. "I need a doctor."

"She's in heat," stated Wesley with dread in his tone. I looked toward him and noticed his pants jutting out in his private area. Same with Tony. They were all turned on at what was happening to me. *What the hell?!*

"We can't," said Grant, shaking his head furiously.

"There's no choice, Grant," said Tony.

I yelped when my pussy clenched painfully. Grant turned to me, a look of stark panic in his eyes. And there was something else. Like a longing he couldn't allow himself to have. I didn't understand what was happening.

"We need to take care of her," said Grant. "Tiana, what we're going to do will seem primitive to you."

"What do you mean?" I asked, panicking.

"When an omega goes into heat, her alphas take turns having sex with her until her heat is over," he explained. My mind went blank in shock. *Is this what my parents were worried about?* This sounded absurd to me.

Absolutely nuts.

"No," I said. "Get out, all of you."

Grant gave Tony a look, and they nodded.

"You won't last too long in this state," said Grant. "One of us will stand outside the room to make sure you don't die or any other complication happens. Shout if it gets worse, and I will be here."

Die?!

"Okay, can you leave now?" I whimpered. He lingered on the side of my bed, gazing at my sweat-covered face, reluctant to leave me. He finally sighed and ordered his pack to leave with him.

Even though I was literally dying in pain with heightened arousal, I wasn't going to do it.

I just met them. I wasn't going to have sex with total strangers. They could be lying, for goodness sake. I'd rather just lay here and wait until the pain passed. One by one, they left the room, and I was left totally alone.

Oh my God, I was going to die here. I couldn't move, and standing up was too painful. I lay in bed in a fetal position as I clenched my eyes tight. I wanted to try calling my mom again.

Grabbing my phone, I dialed her number.

"Tiana?"

"Mom, I'm in a lot of pain," I whispered.

"Are you still on that cruise?"

"Yes, and there are alpha wolves here, too," I said.

"What kind of pain are you in?" asked my mom in a worried tone.

"Like squeezing in my belly. It's unbearable."

"It's because you stopped the heat suppressant pills we gave you," said my mom sharply. *Okay, I didn't need to be yelled at now.* I fully understood now what I did, and it was completely their fault for not warning me.

"You have to mate with the alphas," my dad shouted from the background. "You might die if you don't."

"Listen, Tiana," said Mom. "I know we lied to you about your true self this whole time, but you have to listen to us this one time. If the alphas are willing to help, don't push them away like you do with all your dates."

"Are you freaking serious?" I sighed. My parents were encouraging me to have sex like it was nothing. *They were treating me like I couldn't handle anything my whole life, and now I was okay to have sex with a bunch of alphas?*

"Stopping the pills was a bad idea," said my mom.

"Well, you should have told me before," I grunted when my belly squeezed in pain again. "What if I get pregnant? I never even kissed a guy in my life!"

"I never thought it would come to this," said Mom. "If you get pregnant, you don't have a choice as an omega. I tried my best to protect you. I wanted you to have a choice, but now...I can't do anything for you. You can only hope you can get past this without any repercussions. You are an omega, the rarest kind. I'm sorry, baby."

My pulse pounded in my head, blocking all sounds as I grew dizzy at her words. It was all too unreal.

"I'll...I'll try. Bye, Mom," I said, my heart aching.

"Trust the alphas," said Mom. "They will end up bonding with you, no matter what. When an alpha mates with an omega, his heart is entwined with her forever. Trust me on this."

When she hung up, I dropped my phone with trembling hands.

My innocence was over.

Everything I knew about life was a scam. I didn't have the option to find true love. For an omega, we needed to mate the closest alpha who'd relieve the pain. The thought of having sex with Grant overwhelmed me to the core. I wanted him and didn't want him at the same time.

My mind conflicted with my heart.

The door opened again, and I groaned. *Why couldn't Grant mind his own damn business? Why did he care what was happening to me anyway?*

"Oh no, Tiana, are you still sick?" asked Lori, sitting on her bed and looking at me in concern. I opened my eyes blearily, watching her eat a slice of cake. I was glad it was her and not one of the damn werewolves because I didn't trust myself. I knew I'd cave into having sex with one of them just to relieve this monstrous pain.

"I think it's the flu," I said, feeling another spasm rock through me.

"There's a security guard outside our room," whispered Lori. "The one that you kissed. Did you see him again?"

"I mean, we talked for a bit," I said.

"Ooh, talked?" she asked with a gleam in her eyes. When I didn't smile, she got the message that I wasn't playing around. "Do you need something to eat or drink? Is it your period?"

"No," I said, holding my belly and curling up further in the sheets. "Do you have pain medicine?"

"Yeah, I have some medicine," she said, pulling her backpack from beneath the bed. "My cousin had the nerve to ask me to change into a better dress. I can't believe her. I'll never go to another function of hers again."

"Oh, did she?" I asked, blearily unable to think straight,

After taking the medicine, I closed my eyes to get some sleep.

It was going to be a long and painful night.

———

I WOKE up to a hand pressed to my mouth. Panicked, my eyes shot open.

The room was dark, and night had fallen. I lifted my hands to try and shove the hand away from my mouth. The hand was rock solid.

I couldn't see who it was either. The person was behind me, but I could feel the tough, muscled chest and knew it was one of the alphas.

I felt his energy coursing through my skin, electrifying me. I struggled weakly against him as he lifted me in his arms, his hand still pressed against my mouth. I couldn't scream, and I felt immobile with pain. I was at the complete mercy of whoever was kidnapping me.

As he quietly walked down the hallway and up the stairs, I punched his chest, but it felt like a brick wall. I couldn't look up to see who was carrying me, his hand holding my head in place.

When we reached above deck, I caught sight of Tony and Wesley. So it must be Grant carrying me. *What the hell did he want with me? Were they going to take me by force?*

I bit his hand and screamed when he let go for a second. Then he quickly covered my mouth again.

"Shh, it's for your own good," muttered Grant next to my ear. I shook my head wildly, trying to escape, but he handled me like I was a little doll.

"Let's go," said Tony. "Sam said he's close."

"Hey! What's going on over there?" shouted a voice.

I recognized it as the captain's voice.

"Fuck, we need to jump over," said Grant. "We can't wait for Sam."

Wait, what?!

Before I could scream or do anything to stop it, Grant started racing to the edge of the ship as I bounced in his arms, holding him for dear life.

He jumped overboard with me in his arms. His hand released my mouth at the impact of the cold water, and I screamed.

Oh my god, I wasn't ready to die.

"We need life jackets!" I screamed.

"There's no way," said Grant. Then, suddenly, I felt a sharp, icy pain on my head as I hit the edge of the ship.

Then everything went black.

Ten

GRANT

"Fuck!" I yelled when the icy water hit me. Tiana's unconscious body was draped over my shoulder. She had hit her head hard, and it had all happened in a split second.

It was all my fault. *Please let her be alive...*

I wrapped an arm around her, holding her tight as I swam in the water.

"Grant!" shouted Tony, his long hair drenched from the water as he swam over to us. "What happened to her?"

I tapped her face repeatedly. "Wake up, Tiana!"

Her body was still, but she was breathing.

"What happened?" growled Tony, pushing Tiana's hair away from her face.

"She hit her head when I jumped," I explained, rubbing her cheeks to warm them.

"Damn."

"Where's Wes?" I asked, scanning the perimeter of the water. My body was shivering and cold as I looked around. My teeth were chattering out of control. A werewolf didn't belong in water like this.

"Over there," said Tony. Wesley was swimming over to us.

"Let's swim towards Howl's Edge," I said. "We'll meet Sam on the way since he was coming to get us with his boat."

"How will Sam find us?" asked Wesley.

"We're a pack. He'll know," I said. "Let's go."

I was adapting to the water already. We werewolves weren't built like humans. We had the stamina to survive something like this. But I had a sinking feeling that we could be swimming forever. The waves kept pushing me back, hurling my body in every direction. I lost my phone on the ship, and I was getting disoriented the more we swam away from the ship. I swiped the water from my eyes, trying to see clearly.

I lifted Tiana off my shoulder. I tapped her face and pinched her cheek.

"Tiana, wake up, please," I begged. I was getting more and more worried as more time passed. She was still unconscious, her head lolling to the side.

I gently set her back down on my shoulder.

"It's getting darker without the ship lights," said Tony. "Shit."

"We just need to keep swimming," said Wesley.

I shook the water from my face, trying to stay alert for Sam's boat and to keep from drowning. I know he was out there somewhere. We had agreed to grab Tiana and jump into Sam's boat. I had no idea why Sam wasn't around right now.

After swimming for what seemed like an hour, I heard the engine of a boat.

Finally. My arms were losing strength.

I felt Tiana moving and struggling against me. I lifted her and patted her back as she spat out water. She coughed uncontrollably, gathering the attention of the men.

"You okay, Tiana?"

"I...I think so. We're still in the water. Are we going to die?" she inquired weakly, looking around. I felt sorry for the poor girl. She just wanted a vacation from her parents, and now she was stuck in a cold ass ocean. Her hair was soaked, and she was shivering against me.

And she was in active heat.

"Yes. But we're almost out of here."

"I hear something," said Wesley. "Look, there's a boat not too far away. Probably Sam."

"Sam, is that you?" I yelled.

The boat's engine died, and I could see Sam's head sticking out over the edge. His familiar red bandana wrapped around his head, prominent under the moonlight.

Thank god he was here. My arms were heavy and felt like logs, about to give out.

"Get on board!" Sam yelled, throwing out a rope ladder.

It took the rest of my strength to haul myself up along with Tiana, whose arms were wrapped around my neck, holding on for dear life.

Once we were on the boat, I set her down. My entire body felt drained as I collapsed to my knees for a moment to regain my strength. I noticed Tiana shivering uncontrollably, hunched on the boat floor, and holding her belly. Tony and Wesley piled onto the boat, falling over each other in exhaustion. I knew they were pushed to their limits today.

No one could have foreseen what was coming. We weren't prepared.

"You found the lost omega," said Sam in wonder as he stared at her.

"Get those wet clothes off her," I ordered. The men scrambled over to her while she looked at me, shocked.

"No, get away!" she yelled, but she didn't have the strength to fight them off. Sam lifted her wet dress off her.

"It's to save you," said Wesley, purring into her ear. His purring calmed her as they helped her strip off the cold, wet clothes.

I grabbed a blanket from the stockpile on the lower floor of the boat and ran back to meet them. She was completely naked, and her brown skin glowed under the moon. I stood for a moment, admiring her body.

She looked like something fierce, standing in the wind and glaring at all of us.

I wrapped the blanket around her and peeled off my wet clothes. Naked, I hugged her blanket-wrapped body to me. She was so cold.

Tony and Wesley were filling Sam in on what had happened.

"It hurts so bad," she whimpered in my ear, and a wave of protective instinct overcame me. She was shivering and weak, her legs shaking. I immediately pulled her onto my naked lap to warm her. The wind slapped against my back, goosebumps rising from my skin in the cold. Werewolves didn't get cold as easily, but the swim in the ocean was brutal.

Slowly I was starting to warm up with Tiana's body over mine. My foggy mind was getting clearer, and I was focusing on her now as I began to recover. We sat like that for twenty minutes, with me cuddling her on my lap, getting her warmed up.

She shouted in pain, holding her belly.

"What's going on with me?" she asked breathlessly. "It feels horrible."

"We need to mate with her," said Sam urgently, feeling her forehead. "What the hell were you guys doing with her on the ship? You've brought her heat on with your pheromones."

"Nothing," I said. I knew fingering Tiana would have helped bring her heat on, but I would never admit that. It was hard seeing her suffer with no relief.

"Apparently," said Sam sarcastically, unwrapping the blanket from her and exposing her bare body.

"What are you doing?" she said, her voice low and in pain. Her arms flailed weakly, trying to push Sam away.

"Relax," I whispered, pulling her closer to my lap. "We're going to take care of you. You're in heat now, and your body needs to be filled with our knot."

"What do you mean?"

"We're going to go inside you," I explained clearly. "Like have sex with you and knot inside you."

Eleven

TIANA

Oh my goodness, the pain was too much.

Everything was a haze, and I didn't have the energy to fight off the new guy on the boat as he spread my legs.

"A knot?" I protested, even though the idea sounded very appealing right about now. "I don't know you!"

"You'll have sex with all of us. This is Sam, also part of my pack," explained Grant slowly next to my ear. My ears were waterlogged, but I was sure I heard what he was saying.

"That's crazy," I gasped when another wave of pain shot through me.

"I know it sounds crazy, Tiana," said Grant. "It's just how it is with omegas and alphas. The longer you go without the knot, the sicker you'll become. You could even die."

Wetness seeped from my core, squeezing me again in vicious pain.

"Are you scared?" Sam asked me, kneeling and looking at me with kind eyes.

"Yes," I gasped out as my pussy throbbed with need. Despite my cold skin, my body felt like it was on fire.

"Do you trust me?" he asked while his hand was on my naked leg.

My body was wracked with pain, and unbearable heat spiraled in my belly. Clenching and releasing furiously. Wetness gushed from between my legs with no remorse. I needed something inside me to relieve the pain. Something thick to stop my pussy walls from clenching tightly. Maybe they knew more about this than I did.

"Yes, I trust you," I said, even though deep down I didn't yet.

Wesley sat beside me, rubbing my arm and purring in my ear to calm me. I appreciated his effort, but it did nothing to stop the damn heat going through my body. I wanted an alpha to fuck me senseless.

And the sound of a knot was appealing to me. A thick, juicy knot deep inside of me.

"Open," said Sam, spreading my knees apart.

The instinct to trust him came over me. It was like my omega body knew what it needed, begging me to stop fighting.

"Okay," I whispered, allowing my thighs to relax open for him.

Grant held me on his lap as Sam gazed at me. My face heated, being exposed to a group of guys like this. Never in a million years did I believe this would happen. Sam leaned down between my legs, his red bandana brushing my inner thighs as he looked at my pussy.

"She's full of slick. Definitely in heat," he said, probing me with his fingers. *Oh my*, it felt amazing feeling his fingers touch me like that, opening me up as he inspected me.

My belly contracted again at his touch. Desperation grew inside me.

"Please," I said breathlessly as another wave of pain slammed over me. "I need some kind of relief."

"Go ahead, Sam," ordered Grant. "You can go first. We just got out of the freezing water, so our cocks need time to warm up."

"Okay," said Sam, unbuckling his belt immediately.

I was scared but also didn't want to die. This person, who I'd only known for a couple of minutes, was going to be my first-ever experience with sex.

He had an earring in one ear, and his shirt was ripped in several places. Sam dropped his pants to the floor, and his dick sprang free. I looked at it, surprised at its girth and nearly salivating as I gazed at him.

The sky was dark, and the wind was still strong, rocking the boat.

Grant cupped my breasts as I lay on his lap. I was used to his touch and welcomed it. It distracted me from the horrible pain of my heat.

"Do you care if I play with your breasts while Sam is inside you?" he asked.

"No," I said. "I think it might help."

I could feel Grant's dick hardening underneath my ass as I lay on his lap.

My arousal heightened as he played with my boobs, squeezing and flicking my hard nipples. The wind felt good on my heated pussy, the air brushing past my labia and heated folds.

My legs were sprawled open, waiting for Sam's cock to enter me as he touched my thighs to prepare me. I moaned as more slick seeped down my legs in preparation for his entrance.

Twelve

SAM

Tiana was ready and spread out in front of me.

I wasn't prepared for this when they hopped on my boat. I thought I'd pick them up, and we'd drop her off at Howl's Edge with her new pack. I wasn't ready for this type of immediate connection. The rule was that she wasn't ours, and we weren't supposed to form a connection.

How could I live with myself giving her away after mating?

"I'm going to go inside you. Is that okay?" I asked, holding her thigh open. "You're so beautiful. So wet and needy for me." My balls were heavy, and my dick was hard as fuck. Her musky strawberry scent filled my senses, nearly sending me into a rut. I needed to rut her tonight.

"Yes," she whispered, her thighs shaking. I could tell she was nervous. Her pussy shined under the moonlight, covered in slick. Weeping for us.

Her heated slit became wetter at my words as I slowly rubbed my dick against her pussy, coating it in her slick. My cock was rock hard and pulsing as I gripped it. I nearly groaned at the thought of her warm tight pussy bucking underneath me as I plunged into her.

"Hurry," she begged, widening her legs.

I aligned my cock with her entrance, kneeling on the boat's floor. Rubbing my cock some more against her slick, I pushed inside of her, relishing how she hugged my cock.

I instantly stopped, noticing a barrier blocking my cock from going further. I pulled back immediately.

"I'm a virgin," she said in a low voice.

Oh fuck.

"I didn't know. I'm sorry," I said. "I would have been gentler."

"Please just do it hard," she begged. Tears flowed down her cheeks. "I heard the first time's painful, so keep going. Please."

Her life was in danger. I couldn't play around.

I plunged into her, breaking her hymen in one go. She let out a yelp, and Wesley rushed over to help. He started fingering her clit as I thrust into her slowly. Her pussy walls relaxed around my cock as he strummed her little round nub while Grant squeezed her breasts. Her face was no longer twisted in pain as I continued to thrust. She was so beautiful, spread out under the moonlight.

Then seeing that she was enjoying it, the way she looked at me- I thrust faster into her tight pussy.

The boat rocked, and she gasped as my dick sunk deeper inside her because of the movement.

Fuck...she was tight. *And it was hot.*

I hadn't jacked off in days, and this felt like heaven. I couldn't get enough as I thrust harder into her. My penis hardened even more, and my hips bucked against her as I exploded inside her. My white hot liquid streamed into her, directly into her womb.

I kissed her on the lips as my cock swelled, knotting her. She breathed against my lips, kissing me back.

"Thank you," she said. "I feel so much better already. Why is your penis swelling inside me? I can't move."

"It's called the knot, honey," I explained, realizing she knew nothing about our kind. "When an alpha has sex with an omega, our dick knots and holds you in place for impregnation."

"I don't want to be pregnant!" she protested, trying to pull away from my thick knot. The more she tried to pull away, it suctioned her to me tighter. It was impossible to break the physical bond that held us. And she was going to have to know this. Grant's arms circled her chest, holding her.

"It's rare for omegas to get pregnant on their first heat cycle," I explained to calm her frantic efforts. Her efforts were tugging my cock, causing the knot to harden even faster. It was nature's way of ensuring we procreated and only omegas could handle our knots without being in pain.

"It's very rare," assured Grant, purring in her ear. "Relax and let his knot finish pumping inside you. This is the mating process."

"What happens if I get pregnant, though?" she asked, panicking.

"We'll take care of you. No matter what," said Grant.

"Okay. I guess I don't have a choice, huh? Either get knotted by you or die in pain," said Tiana sarcastically as she wiggled around my knot. "Why don't you wear condoms?"

"Huh?" I asked. That sounded foreign to me, and I've never heard of that.

"Umm, protection," she explained. "Like a rubber over your cock to prevent pregnancy."

"Why would I want to prevent having a baby?" I asked, confused. An alpha's goal was to form a pack and breed his omega. The ultimate joy was seeing her belly swell with child.

"The condom would break over your knot anyway," she sighed, closing her eyes as she lay underneath me on Grant's lap. My knot was nice and snug into her as she closed her eyes in bliss. "Is the pain going to come back when you're done?"

"It will," I said, feeling sorry for this poor omega. She had no idea how this worked, growing up with humans and having a messed version of sex. She was going to learn soon.

"Oh no," she groaned at the thought of the impending pain.

"But don't worry, I'm not going anywhere, honey," I said. "As soon as my knot goes down, one of the other guys will take over and knot inside you next."

"Okay," she said, wrapping her arms around me and kissing my neck, to my surprise. Her tears of relief brushed against my ear. "Sorry, I know I just met you, but you helped so much."

Her face looked embarrassed as she released me, and my heart swelled ten sizes. It was dangerous that she was bonding so quickly, and I could see Grant's eyes flash with utter panic.

Thirteen

TIANA

Relief at last.

I knew it would be short-lived, but I felt so much better as Sam pushed his knot further inside of me. His heat and alpha energy flowed through me, invigorating me. I was sandwiched between Sam and Grant. Sam was on top of me, and Grant was underneath as I lay across his lap.

I felt Grant's dick stirring under my ass, so I knew I was covered.

"Am I just going to be a sex-starved fiend for the rest of my life?" I asked sadly.

"No, you'll only go into heat every few months," said Wesley, who stripped off his wet clothing and wore simple pants that he found on the boat. "We don't know how your body will work. Every omega is different."

"This changes my whole life," I said.

I tried to pull away from Sam, but his knot held me in place, locking me underneath him. He pushed my hair away from my face.

"Relax," he said, purring in my ear. I felt a calmness go through me under his purring. However, as soon as the knot began to deflate, I felt the pain in my womb start to rise again from the emptiness.

"How long will I be in heat for?" I asked in a panic.

"A week tops," said Tony, squeezing water from his long black hair.

"What?!" I said.

I couldn't imagine going through this for another day. Let alone a week. The alphas looked at me like I was their next meal, and I warmed under their gazes.

"That's why an omega must have multiple mates to help her," said Grant. It was starting to make more sense to me after feeling the relief Sam gave me. Being an omega sucked, and I wondered what would have happened if I had stopped the pills and the alphas weren't around me.

"Who's up next?" said Sam. "I'm about to pull out here."

Sam's knot was starting to release me, and a wave of panic went through me when my belly started to contract again.

"I'll take her next," said Grant, laying me on a blanket as Sam climbed off me, kissing me on the lips. My eyes fluttered at his warm lips, glad this wasn't as cold and clinical as I thought it might be.

Sam pulled his pants back on and went to steer the boat, taking over from Wesley.

My pussy clenched in anticipation as I watched Grant climb over me next, spreading my knees apart. I've wanted him since he touched me on the cruise ship.

Grant leaned down, bringing his face to mine. He kissed me square on the lips, his sideburns brushing against my skin. I kissed him back, feeling his warm lips over mine. His tongue pushed into my mouth, tasting me. Taking me like he owned me. I sighed underneath him, opening my legs wider for him as heat coursed through my body.

I burned with a need to have him inside of me. Deep inside.

"Grant, I need you," I said, my vulnerability showing in my voice. I hated being vulnerable. But my inner omega rejoiced at finally being her true self.

"What do you call me again?" he growled in my ear.

"Alpha, I need you," I said, knowing what he wanted to hear.

"Your wish is my command, sweetheart."

His dick was thick and veiny as it loomed over me. I couldn't help but freeze at how thick it looked. Wrapping my fingers around it, I slowly guided him inside me. I squirmed, trying to get the entire length to go in easily. He pinned me down under him with his massive physique and strength, and I couldn't help but admire how his chest and abs shone in the dark. I grabbed his upper arms as he pushed all the way inside me.

"You're too big," I gasped. "But it feels so good."

"Good," he said, plunging deep inside my tightness. "You're so tight, baby."

With my slick and Sam's semen still inside me, my pussy was plenty lubricated enough for his cock. Grant smelled like the ocean with his musky wood odor underneath. He smelled intoxicating to me.

My pussy stretched around his dick, clenching tight. Never wanting to let go.

Grant pumped inside of me, filling me like I'd never been filled before. Tony leaned down and started kissing my neck while playing with my clitoris.

I never had sex with one man, let alone more than one, trying to pleasure me. I tried not to feel self-conscious when they crowded around me, blocking the wind and staring at my naked body.

Wesley sucked on my breasts and licked my nipples while Grant repeatedly thrust into me.

A whirl of fireworks coursed through my body, and my

pussy clenched tight as I came. My back arched, and my legs fell open wider as I climaxed. Grant roared as my pussy hugged his cock. Then he came not long after. Shots of his cum spurted inside of me.

His cock swelled inside of me, filling me nicely. I laid there, spent and content. I hugged him to me as he lay on top of me.

"Thank you," I said.

"Don't thank me," he said. "An alpha must protect and mate an omega. It's just..."

He suddenly stopped talking. Looking away from me.

"What's wrong?" I asked.

All the men were on alert, waiting for what he'd say next. It was quiet for a few minutes, and my heart was racing from the tension in the air.

Why was he acting like this? Was sex with me that bad?

All my insecurities were starting to surface.

"I don't know if it's the right time to tell you this. But you need to know, and I can't keep going on like this," he said, looking down at our privates connected with his knot.

"Not now, Grant," warned Wesley.

"I don't care, tell me," I said, adrenaline going through me. I was scared and nervous about what he was going to say.

"I'm not taking you home, and you're not going to be the omega of our pack," he said.

"Wait, wait, wait," I said. "Slow down a minute. You're not taking me home, so where are you taking me?"

"To Howl's Edge Island," he said.

"Why are you taking me there if you don't want me to be with you?" I said, trying to think logically before I let my emotions take over. "Why not just take me back home?"

"I made a deal with another pack. They want you, and I will drop you off to them," he said.

Rejection shot through me like a knife. My chest began to hurt with his admission.

Why was he telling me at the worst time? *While he was still inside of me?* I could see Tony shaking his head in disappointment with Grant.

"Why?" I said, tears welling in my eyes. "Why would you do that to me?"

"It has to be done. I'm only telling you so you can protect your heart," he said coldly.

"You're a damn asshole," I said. "You all are!"

I looked over at the others. Their heads were bowed. No one had the nerve to even look at me. I felt duped and ashamed. Why did they have sex with me? Why did Grant come into the bathroom and finger me?

I tried to pull away from his knot, but it locked me in place. I wanted to be anywhere else but here.

I wanted out.

As soon as Grant's knot released me, I slapped him in the face as white-hot rage coursed through me. As I lay there, knotted up, I waited until it released me.

He blinked, startled.

"Why do you look so surprised?" I shouted. I grabbed the blanket and wrapped it around my naked body. "You're here trading me off like it's a normal thing. Like I don't matter at all. Like I don't have a family. How could you?!"

"Listen, I'm sorry," said Grant, reaching for me, but I quickly stepped away from him.

I walked to the corner of the boat next to a bunch of barrels - wrapping the blanket around me as I sat there away from them all. I stared out at the waters, unable to believe what just happened. A swirl of pain went through my belly, but I didn't care now. I'd rather die than sleep with Grant and his men ever again. I hoped to god I wasn't pregnant either, or else that would be a disaster for sure.

I could see Tony staring at me a few feet away, harshly whispering to Grant. Wesley's eyes were downcast as he shook his head in disappointment at Grant. None of them were happy with his decision.

The ocean was dark, and a sliver of fear coursed through me, thinking the boat could topple over at any time. I groaned as the heat within my body worsened, needing another knot. I didn't care. I needed to ignore it as much as possible.

"Tiana?" said Tony, coming near me. I kept my eyes on the water, ignoring his hulking presence. "I know you're in pain. Let me help you, baby."

Tears pricked my eyes as my stomach contracted again.

"Just go away," I whispered shakily. I needed his knot desperately, but it was so wrong. He came over to my side and touched my back. The warmth of his hand sent shivers down my back. His alpha scent called to me, begging my inner omega to bury my nose in his neck and allow him to take care of me.

"Let me help you. Just think of it as a one-night stand," said Tony. I wasn't surprised he knew the term since he lived in North America, stalking me. "All you need is a knot to help you get through this. We don't agree with Grant's decision at all to give you away to another pack."

"Then why are you helping him?"

"He's the pack leader," said Tony, his voice withdrawn. I looked at him and noticed he was staring up at the moon in thought. "I have a feeling it won't be easy for him to give you up just like that. Not when we spent half our lives searching for you."

"I don't even want to be with him," I protested. "I just want to go home."

"Then I'll do everything in my power to make sure that

happens. Whatever you want, Tiana," said Tony, and I bit my lip, looking at him. "I will try to convince Grant that it's not a good idea to take you like this. I promise I'll try. Just let me help you."

The pain was getting unbearable with each passing second while slick seeped from my pulsing core.

"Just keep Grant away from me," I said, letting the blanket fall open around me, exposing myself to him. His eyes darkened as he gazed at my hanging breasts and dark pubic hair as I sat there.

"I'll keep him far away from you," said Tony hoarsely as he stripped off his jeans. I noticed Sam, Wesley, and Grant were looking at us from the corner of my eye as I lay on the floor of the boat, spreading my legs for Tony. He climbed on top of me, his cock swinging between his legs as he lowered his head to mine. Then he whispered in my ear. "Just pretend it's you and me. Enjoy my knot inside you, baby."

"Okay," I breathed, turning my gaze to him as he pushed inside of me. My pussy stretched wider and wider the more he inserted his cock inside of me, and it felt amazing from this beautiful man.

"Do you like my cock inside your tight little pussy?"

"Yes."

"I like it too, Tiana. I'm going to fuck your hot little cunt. Are you ready?"

"Please, Tony," I begged, wriggling my hips for him to move. He chuckled darkly as he pumped his cock into me. Long, deep thrusts that sent me flying. I groaned loudly as I felt my climax emerging as he hit my sensitive spot over and over, his cock curving upwards. It was nothing like I felt before.

"Sam and Grant stretched you out nicely for me," he observed, biting my earlobe as his hips pistoned into me. My pulse raced, and my breathing accelerated as he fucked me in the night on the tiny wobbly boat.

"Oh, Tony," I moaned. My stomach tensed, and I saw fireworks as I shattered around his thick cock.

"Good girl," he said, groaning at his own impending climax. His thick pulsing cock, pressed deep within me when he exploded inside of me, shooting his load of hot semen. I was excited to feel the knot again, and I opened my legs wider to receive him. "That's a good omega. Keep your legs open like that for me. So tight and moist."

He pressed his hands underneath my thighs to keep me wide open as his cock swelled more and more. I gasped at the thickness of it and the relief it brought me. It was instant relief from my heat, his cock keeping me stretched fully as I lay underneath him.

"Your knot," I gasped as he nibbled my neck.

"Doesn't that feel good, little omega?" he asked.

"Yes," I said. "Can we just lay like this forever?"

His gaze darkened, and I realized the mistake I made. He wasn't going to be around me after we got to the island. It was just so easy for me to feel attached like this, and I needed to get a grip.

"Sorry," I said quickly.

"It's okay. I wish more than ever that it can happen," he said. "One day, little omega."

Fourteen

GRANT

Stepping off the boat, I took in the bright sun and morning breeze.

I took it all in as I stood on the beach of Howl's Edge. It was like I had never left the place.

The familiar statue of the giant wolf holding our flag in his mouth greeted us. I smelled the amazing fresh air and took in the sight of the beautiful palm trees surrounding the island.

My heart was heavy as I looked back at the boat.

Tiana wouldn't allow us to touch her anymore, and it was time to drop her off to her new pack right away before her body went into shock from her heat.

She stood on the beach in her bare feet and wrinkled emerald dress. She had streaks of eyeliner down her face from crying all night on the boat. The only person she let near her was Tony and sometimes Wesley. She had a connection with Tony that I'd never understand. I was the one who saw her first. I shook my head, annoyed at myself.

I was about to give her away, so I needed to stick to my word as leader alpha of this pack. I couldn't change my mind and look weak.

"What have you got there, sir?" said a voice. I turned, seeing a group of security betas who patrolled the shore approaching us.

"This is my pack and an omega," I said. Sam and Wesley came up to stand on either side of me. Tony was carrying Tiana in his arms, standing off to the side, watching what was going on. The beta pulled out a clipboard and a pen. He looked at all of us, studying the way Tiana clung to Tony.

"Pack name?" he said, his eyes scrolling down a list of names on his paper. I hated security here, but I knew it was necessary.

"Frostcrown," I answered.

"Your pack isn't registered with an omega. Unfortunately, we'll need to take this omega in for custody so she's not taken advantage of," he said, scratching his large orange mustache.

"She's not ours. I'm taking her to a different pack who made an offer for her," I said.

"And what pack is that?"

"The Lustfur Pack."

The beta's eyes instantly widened, and he set his clipboard down.

"Alright, looks like everything is in order then," he said hastily. Then he turned to Tiana. "Good luck. If anything goes south with your new pack, don't hesitate to reach out."

He handed her a card, and she took it without a word. The beta security guards walked down the shore to harass another group of people.

"You sure this is the right choice, boss?" asked Sam as he tightened his bandana in frustration. I knew all the men were upset with me. Especially Sam since he was the first to mate with her and take her virginity.

"I stick to my word with the other packs," I said. "I'll lose all respect and my side of the deal."

We walked across the beach.

It seemed more barren, empty, and lifeless now. I barely spotted any females around here. There were lots more boats and construction now on the island. We passed by giant palm trees, and I plucked a date from one of them, chewing on one as I walked.

"Are we taking her right now?" asked Sam.

"Yes, she's in pain. She needs to go to her pack right now," I stressed. "The decision is final."

I have been the leader of the pack since I started it more than twenty years ago. I met Sam, an outcast on the streets like myself, and we decided to form a pack recruiting Tony and Wesley.

I looked back and saw Tony still carrying the little omega in his arms, cradling her like she was going to break. He looked up, glaring at me.

I sighed.

"The men aren't happy with this decision," pressed Sam.

"I know, goddamn it," I growled. "We're here now."

We stopped in front of the giant mansion which held the most powerful pack on Howl's Edge. The mansion was lined with gold, and the door knobs were also gold. Sometimes, I wonder how they got so wealthy, but I wasn't one to ask too many questions. This pack did a lot of fishy business. At the sight of the home, I felt a sinking dread in my stomach.

This was the last time I'd see Tiana.

I waved Tony over, and then Tony dumped her in my arms in vengeance.

"You can be the one to do the dirty job," he spat out. Then he kissed Tiana on the lips one last time, and she clung to him, tears in her eyes. "Be a good girl. They'll take care of you. You even have a mansion, nothing like we could ever give you."

"I don't care about material things," she sobbed.

"Tony, you're making this harder than it is," I said, although my heart physically hurt.

He knew it would hurt me more if I got to touch her and then have her taken away. My annoyance soon disappeared, feeling her soft, curvy bottom in my arms. Her sweet strawberry scent was intoxicating. I breathed it in one last time despite her anger. She didn't even look me in the eyes. Her face was turned the entire time, trained on the large mansion.

I wondered what was going through her mind.

I rang the doorbell. And waited.

Fifteen

TIANA

I hated Grant at this moment. There was no way I would ever forgive him after this.

"I can stand," I insisted, even though my abdomen clenched in pain. His arms wrapped tighter around me.

"I know you're in pain, and I know you have your pride," he argued.

Just then, the double doors opened. A man wearing a purple robe answered the door. He looked to be in his forties, and it looked like he had dyed his long hair white. His purple eyes looked crazy as he looked at us. His thin lips pulled up in a smile.

I grew wary of him at first sight.

"Grant! After all these years," he said. Then his eyes zeroed in on me. "You've brought her to me. Very nice."

"I expect you to keep your end of the deal, Jatix," said Grant in a serious tone. "I lived on the human lands tracking her down for years, and now I expect my property and orchard."

I couldn't believe him.

He was trading me in for property. This was the plan years

ago. Grant was conniving, and he was getting riches while I was going to be the property of this pack.

Jatix couldn't keep his eyes off me. His hands pawed my arms and elbows, feeling me up like his toy. My stomach turned.

"Stop," I seethed. "I don't want to be with any pack."

Jatix laughed, holding his knees.

"She's been living on the human lands too long and raised like a regular human. She doesn't know she belongs with a pack," he said breathlessly. "Grant, I'll sit with you tomorrow morning to write the check and all the property you own."

"I'll never forgive you," I seethed, staring daggers at Grant.

Grant slowly set me down on my feet and touched the small of my back.

"This is goodbye, then," said Grant. That was the only thing he could say.

I couldn't turn to look at him. I just couldn't.

"Just go," I choked out. My life was falling apart.

Why couldn't I sit my ass at home? I should never have gone on the cruise ship.

"Come with me, sweetheart," said Jatix, holding my hand and bringing me inside the mansion. Women were hanging around everywhere, and men were fawning over them in different positions. The women were soon forgotten when the pack turned to look at me. I noticed some of the women looking angry and jealous at my arrival. "Men! I brought a surprise."

Before I could even blink, four other men surrounded me.

"She's an omega," said one of the guys. He had a bunch of piercings. They were all looking at me in wonder and enthrall-ment. "I could smell her omega scent."

"Yes, she sure is an omega," said Jatix.

"I'm not your omega!" I said, backing away from them. They all looked frightening, with Jatix being the worst with his crazy eyes. All those tattoos and hard muscles surrounding me were way too intimidating.

"Hmm," said Jatix, stalking me. Eyes narrowed.

My chest rose and fell in shallow breaths as I panicked. I was still in heat, and now I was freaking scared, so it wasn't a good combination. I felt aroused and also shaking with fear. Two alphas looked like twins, with one being chubbier.

"Please let me go," I said.

"It's the law for an omega to mate with alphas," said Jatix. "You cannot survive on your own. Now bring that sweet ass over here before I punish you." His threat wasn't light. It looked like he meant it.

I turned and ran for the front door.

But the pack was too fast for me. Someone grabbed me from behind, lifting me into the air.

"Where do you want her, Jatix?" asked the rough voice of the man carrying me against his scarred chest. The largest male of the pack was holding me.

"To the Naughty Room, Darius," said Jatix. "She tried to run away, so we must train her and teach her a lesson."

What the hell?

I grew increasingly terrified as we descended a flight of stairs.

I fought and shoved the man holding me, but it was like fighting a boulder. He wasn't budging, and his hold on my midsection tightened as he carried me. Finally, after a few minutes of walking down the stairs, the man set me down, and I hitched up my wet dress to keep from tripping.

Jatix pulled my hand into a darkly lit room.

The room had red curtains covering all the windows from top to bottom. In the back, multiple beds were in a neat, straight row covered in white sheets. In the middle of the vast room, contraptions hung from the ceiling. Handcuffs hung from them, and next to them were different-colored whips of varying sizes.

I stared wide-eyed at all the sex toys.

I didn't recognize many sitting on a shelf organized by labels. Vibrators, anal plugs, beads, vibrating panties, and other things that looked like torture devices to me were terrifying. But my body turned hotter as I gazed at them, scared of what Jatix had planned for me.

"What are you going to do to me?" I asked when he sat on a large chair and pulled me onto his lap.

"Before I can share you with my pack, I have to spank you, darling," he said. "Just a warm-up before we get to the show."

"Please don't," I trembled. I was trapped. I tried to pull away from him, but I was no match for his strength.

The four men stood around us like guards, preventing my escape.

Jatix touched my chin in mock pity, his eyes delighted. I looked away. In seconds, he had spun me around, and my bottom was turned to face him. I squirmed and tried to get out of his grasp, but it was useless. My breasts were squashed against his knees, covered in his stupid purple robe. He smelled excessively of cologne.

He pulled up my dress, exposing my butt. I wasn't wearing any underwear. I had lost it on Sam's boat on the way here.

"What a beautiful plump bottom," he said, rubbing his palm over it. "You are ours, little omega. We have been waiting for you for a long time. Right men?"

My heart beat faster, trying to block him out. But the pain from my heat made it impossible to zone out. I needed a knot.

"Yes," one of the men answered in response.

"Who wants to see me open her up?" said Jatix.

"Spread her open, alpha Jatix," said one of the men in a hitched voice. I could hear unzipping and could see their pants start to drop. They were watching me closely, and my pussy was dripping despite my fear.

"First, she needs to be spanked. Right, little omega?" said Jatix.

"No," I said.

That earned me a swift, hard spank to my left buttock.

I yelped in pain. When the sting died down, he spanked me again on the opposite cheek. I squirmed in his lap, trying to rub my aroused pussy on his knee. His spanking made me more aroused, and my womb clenched painfully.

"Such a pretty bottom," said Jatix. "It looks shocked and pink right now. I'll spread you open for my men to take a look. Be a good girl and open up."

I kept my knees together, refusing to open for them.

"I'm not your omega," I stubbornly refused again. I thought about Grant and his rejection of me. I bit my lower lip, refusing to cry.

Suddenly, the door crashed open, and the men quickly pulled their pants up.

"What's going on?" I heard Grant's voice.

"What do you want, Grant?" asked Jatix, patting my ass to stay put. "The deal is done. We get to do whatever we want with *our* omega."

"I reject the offer," said Grant in his booming voice. "I'd like the omega back."

"Ha, it's too late," said Jatix. "She's a pretty little thing, and I actually really like her. You can have any of my beta females upstairs if you want. I don't give a fuck about them."

"I don't want your betas."

"Are you challenging me?"

"I am," said Grant, not hesitating.

Jatix pushed me off his lap, and I scrambled up, pulling my dress down. Jatix tied his robes tighter around him, his body stiff with anger. I saw Wesley, Tony, and Sam enter the room after Grant.

My omega heart sang when I saw Grant and his pack again. Tony winked at me, and I smiled through my tears.

There was hope now. When Grant saw the tears in my eyes, he turned to Jatix. His gaze was ice, and his face twisted up in a savage snarl.

"What's wrong?" taunted Jatix.

"You fucker," Grant growled with all the alpha power in his voice. "You made her cry."

Then he charged at Jatix.

"Back off," screamed Jatix. But Grant was punching him repeatedly in the face.

All hell broke loose, and chaos erupted.

Bodies were being hurled and flying everywhere. The mansion erupted in the sound of shouts and broken furniture.

Tony ran towards me and grabbed my hand.

"I need to get you to safety," he said as we skirted around the fight and ran up the stairs. By the time we made it upstairs, I was out of breath, and I could see the living room had cleared out of all the naked ladies.

Tony opened a random door, and we barricaded ourselves inside the broom closet. There were cleaning supplies, and it smelled like soap and bleach. We were crammed in the tiny space, Tony's large body inches from mine.

"What made Grant come back?" I asked.

"We told him that he was being an asshole," he said. "He ended up caving in when he was finally convinced it wasn't a good idea."

"Wow," I said. Being this close to Tony was causing my arousal to rise again. After the spanking I received today, I was horny again. "Tony, I need some help."

"Yes?" he asked, looking at me knowingly. I knew that he knew.

"Umm, I need relief."

"What kind of relief?"

All day, I was cramping, trying to forget my pain. But now, it had come back with a vengeance.

I held my middle. "It hurts, Tony."

"Lift your dress, baby," he said, quickly unzipping his pants. I hurriedly lifted my dress, exposing myself. I needed him. My body had a mind of its own ever since I stopped taking the pills. The dormant omega inside had come alive.

Tony lifted me up, pressing my back up against the wall. He lifted my legs, and I wrapped them around his waist.

My pussy was aching to be penetrated deep. The fighting downstairs was forgotten.

I was focused on the here and now.

"I'm sorry this is a bad time," I whispered as he pushed his cock inside me. The girth of it stretched my pussy wide.

"Don't apologize, baby," he said, kissing my neck. "My cock feels so good right now. Let me fuck you."

"Harder," I moaned, and he thrust his hips against me, burying deeper inside me. His thumbs flicked my nipples as he pounded into me, stimulating my entire body. His hot breath on my neck and his hair brushing against my arm sent me into a frenzy. I moved my hips along with him, pulling him deeper inside me. My hands scratched the back of his neck when I pulled him in for a kiss.

His tongue pushed into my mouth.

Our tongues twisted over each other wildly as his dick thrust inside me harder and harder.

"I'm gonna come, baby," he said against my mouth. His tongue plundered my mouth as he orgasmed inside me.

"So hot," I whispered, my lips on his. His cock swelled inside me, knotting me to him. I was scared of getting pregnant, but when I was in heat, it was impossible to think clearly except wanting to fuck an alpha.

His hand touched my pussy as his cock was still buried deep inside me, pumping out streams of hot liquid. His large thumb rubbed my clitoris, and I sighed against his lips in pleasure. I was sensitive, and any touch could set me off. I closed my eyes, feeling the pad of his thumb rubbing my clit in an up-and-down motion.

It felt amazing.

My pussy was filled with cock, and the stimulation against my clit was something I had dreamed about even before my heat.

"Come for me, baby," he said. "Your clit is so swollen. I need your slick baby."

"Oh," I moaned. My legs clenched. My pussy tightened over the thick knot, pulling it inside me deeper as my orgasm rocked through my body. My body trembled as he closed his eyes in ecstasy.

We lay in a sweaty mess on the closet floor, waiting for the knot to recede. I played with the hair on his tan chest.

"I want to do this with you forever," Tony said, squeezing and playing with my breasts. My nipple started hardening again as he gently squeezed.

"What's going to happen to me?" I asked.

"You'll be shared with our pack when you live with us," he answered.

"You're not bringing me back home? Will I ever see my parents again?"

"You're an omega. You belong with an alpha pack, your true home," he said matter-of-factly, like it didn't sound outrageous at all. But when he saw the shock on my face, he quickly righted his words. "You can always bring that up to Grant."

We heard crashing, and the knot inside of me was slowly receding in size. I tried to think of a plan. I had to escape this crazy island somehow.

"The fight doesn't look like it's going so well," I whispered. "They might need your help."

"I'm not leaving you," he growled, touching my hair and looking into my eyes. My heart beat faster and faster as I thought of my plan to run.

"I'll be okay," I said. "I won't move from here. If your pack loses, they'll take me."

He licked his lips and silently pulled out of me when his knot released me.

"Stay here until I get back, okay?" he said finally, pulling his jeans back on and buckling his belt.

"Okay."

He left the closet and closed the door behind him.

My pain had eased for the time being. I got up and leaned against the wall, trying to catch my breath.

There was a whirlwind of emotions going through me. I wanted to be part of their pack so badly. To let these alphas take care of me. It was a strange new feeling that I'd never had before.

I thought I'd graduate from college and find a man in my forties one day. But I wasn't prepared for this, and I sure as hell won't be trapped on Howl's Edge forever.

This was my only chance to escape.

I hitched up my dress and slowly opened the door. I peeked out the door.

Seeing no one there, I quickly ran to the front door. In my bare feet, I ran across the front yard and between the palm trees. It was hard running across the warm sand, slowing me down. My heart was pumping wildly with every step I took farther away from the house. I saw a street full of vendors selling things.

I ran down the road, trying not to crash into people. The people on Howl's Edge looked no different than people in my hometown, just scruffier looking. Every once in a while, I'd see a full-blown werewolf strolling in the crowded streets. It was rare to see omegas here, as well. The sun was hot on my back as I weaved my way through the people.

"Five hundred dollars!" shouted a man. I looked over to see what the commotion was about. I was shocked to see a stage with females chained by their ankles standing in a row. They were dressed up in fancy dresses and tons of makeup.

"What in the actual hell?" I muttered to myself, shocked at what I was seeing. *Were they auctioning off females?* This couldn't be real. The females looked unhappy and wouldn't look at the crowd. They all had the same mark on their shoulder.

The wolf claw mark that I had. So they were omegas.

My heart hurt for them, but I was in trouble if I didn't escape off this island fast enough.

Sixteen

GRANT

"You did well," I said to my pack. I was fuckin' proud of them.

Jatix was lying on the ground, gagged with his own bathrobe. And handcuffed to one of the beds.

His men were unconscious on the ground, bloody and wrecked. Four of us against five of them had me worried, but Jatix was far from prepared for a fight, and his men were horny assholes with their pants around their ankles.

"Tiana is upstairs," said Tony after helping us beat the shit out of them.

I wiped the blood off my face using the bottom of my shirt. I didn't want to look too crazy when I saw Tiana again. I had a shit ton of apologizing to do. She was upstairs and waiting for us. I couldn't wait to take her home and claim her as ours. She was ours, and I couldn't wait to tell her.

Wesley ran up the stairs ahead of everyone like a loyal puppy to her, even though he hadn't spent much time with Tiana. I could tell he was awestruck by her. I rolled my eyes but couldn't help but smile at his eagerness. He was the type of guy who wore his emotions on his sleeve.

"Good day, huh?" said Sam, observing me.

"Aside from the fact that we're broke- yes, it's a good day," I said. Sam was my second-hand man, the guy who kept an eye on things on Howl's Edge for me.

"I have bad news," said Tony, his face downcast when we reached the top of the steps.

"What is it?" I said.

"She's not there," he said, his voice controlled. "She promised she'd stay here. She must have run off the first chance she got."

"Oh, did she?" I growled. My hands shook as I slammed the closet door open. It was empty. "We need to find her before any other alphas smell her scent. She's in danger."

"If you didn't throw her away, this would never have happened," said Tony, his hands balled into fists. "If something happens to her, Grant..."

"Then what?" I said, surprised at his challenge.

Tony didn't answer the question as he stalked out the front door in search of Tiana.

"Let's go find her," said Sam. "By the time we kill each other for her, she'll end up in the wrong hands."

I was seething and ready to murder whoever touched my omega.

After searching the island for an hour, we finally found her. Tiana was talking to an older woman with dreadlocks and a necklace of beads all over her neck. The woman was sitting under a palm tree, sitting on top of a rug with her merchandise of jewelry, herbs, and pills sprawled all over it. She was the witch woman of Howl's Edge. I always stayed far away from Zaneesha. The only thing she was useful for was concocting omega pills and any natural medicines that the people needed.

"I'll go to talk to Tiana," said Tony. "You'll only scare her off."

"No, I'll do it," I said, barreling straight in her direction.

It was as if she sensed I was coming toward her.

Tiana immediately turned and started running between the palm trees.

I chased her. She was swift, but I was faster. She was holding up her dress, showing off her thick, shapely thighs. The wolf in me was thrilled to chase this omega.

To earn his prize.

My legs pumped harder, catching up with her.

"Tiana!" I shouted, grabbing her arm. She fell, and I rolled underneath her to soften her fall, pulling her on top of me.

"Let me go!" she gasped, punching my chest with her small fists. I rolled around, pinning her under me. I could smell her musky omega scent. It drove my wolf crazy smelling her. I was already acquainted with her scent of arousal.

My hardened cock pressed against her belly.

Seventeen

TIANA

I wiggled and squirmed, trying to get out. I couldn't believe they had found me so easily.

"I'm sorry, Tiana," Grant said gruffly.

"Sorry for what? For kidnapping or selling me as a sex slave to a psycho werewolf?" I demanded, breathless and getting tired of him.

There was a muscle-packed werewolf on top of me. And it was hard to think clearly under the hot sun.

He was looking at me intently, probably hoping I'd forgive him easily.

"I'm sorry for everything," he replied. "I made a mistake. I signed up to get you because I grew up poor my whole life on this island. I'm serious when I say this, Tiana. I'll never disappoint you again or put you in harm's way. Ever again."

"What do you mean you 'signed up to get me'?"

"Years ago, it was big news when a midwife was charged for not registering a baby to Howl's Edge. She finally confessed that the parents had run away and they had an omega child," he said.

"What do you mean?"

"It's the law for every baby to be registered on the island to be accounted for. So they can keep track of omegas. Jatix was twenty back then and announced to the island that he would give away mansions and land to anyone who found the omega."

"Why?" I asked. To me, that sounded creepy as fuck. "Why did he want me? An omega?"

"Omegas are scarce," said Grant. "I know that's not a good reason, but maybe Jatix thought he could put you up for auction. Omegas can fetch hefty prices, especially the prettier ones. I would never know his reason, but I was willing to bring him an omega if it meant not worrying about money for the rest of my life. We were tired of living on the streets."

"I just passed by an auction. It was the craziest thing I've ever seen. That shouldn't be legal!"

"Auctions are still legal. Bride kidnappings are illegal, though."

"It doesn't sound much better at all," I said, confused. "It needs to be banned. Omegas are being treated like second-class citizens."

"I know," said Grant. "Every alpha on Howl's Edge wants an omega for their pack. So the parents who sell their omega daughter or son would rather be compensated big than giving them away for free."

"I was just walking around the island like it was nothing. Anyone could have taken me," I said, remembering my close call. I was passing by so many people, and they could've snatched me up.

"You have our scent on you. You just mated with Tony," winked Grant. "Once you are taken and mated by an alpha pack, other alphas know to stay away."

"I guess that's good to know," I said, still confused. This island seemed so primitive to me. It didn't feel safe to live here.

He sat up, lifting his body weight off of me, which was

making me flustered. I sat up as well, not touching him. I was still upset he had put me in this position.

"Listen, I'm not trying to pressure or force you," Grant said. "I want you to know that I'm sorry."

I looked around, seeing the rest of the men surrounding us. *Could I forgive Grant?* He kidnapped me, and I wanted to be in his arms for no logical reason.

They were waiting for my answer.

"I forgive you," I said, looking away from him and staring at the ocean waves instead. "But I want to go home. I can't trust you."

Grant tilted my chin to face him. His sensual hooded eyes looked into mine. Studying me.

My core heated and clenched as we made eye contact. I could feel his hard cock pressing against my thigh. He touched my left breast, feeling my wildly beating heart.

"You have a point. But does the little omega wolf inside you trust me?" he asked in a serious tone. His question sounded ridiculous to my ears, but I could feel my inner omega come alive. It was like a second subconscious within me, softly whispering to take him back.

To give him my soul and body.

I wanted him to claim me.

To take me.

"Grant," I sighed, tears spilling down my cheeks. "They hurt me. The pack you gave me to. I felt like garbage. I felt...I felt so small."

Grant sat up and pulled me to him, wrapping his muscular arms around me. I cried against his chest, my tears streaming down my face.

I felt instantly safe in his arms and against his bare chest. He touched my hair and rubbed my shoulder, purring all the while. His vibrations was calming against my racing heart.

"I'm so sorry," he said over and over, hugging me tightly.

Rocking and cradling me in his lap. He was so big and comforting. I felt the protective instinct emanating from his alpha soul.

After a few minutes of crying, I tried to get it together. I sniffed, wiping my nose with the back of my hand, wishing I had a tissue.

"It's okay," I hiccuped, looking at the calming ocean. "But if you do it again, I don't want to be around you. Ever."

"I promise you," said Grant. "Trust me. It sounds like too much right now, but over time, all I can do is prove myself."

We sat silently for a few minutes as he held me against his chest. My tears began to dry on my cheeks, and I felt a lot calmer now. Peace came over my body. I was scared to trust Grant again, but I wanted to give him one more chance. Even though he betrayed me, my inner omega craved to trust him.

I wanted him. And his pack.

"Will you be our omega?" asked Tony, plopping down next to us.

I let out a soft laugh and took his outstretched hand. His large, warm hand encircled mine, rubbing his thumb over my hand.

"I'll try," I said. "If you'll have me and if we see my parents again."

"That's a promise," said Grant.

Tony leaned over, regardless of Grant, and kissed me squarely on the lips. I smiled and kissed him back. When our kiss ended, Grant kissed me next.

As I kissed him back, my heart seemed to grow ten sizes in wonder and excitement. Four men wanted my attention, and I was going to have a lot of love around me.

"Oh my," I said breathlessly when our intense kiss ended with all the men watching us.

"And you'll be getting a lot more than that as soon as I rent us a spot on this island," said Grant, pulling my hand over his pants. I smiled, shocked that I could make a man so easily aroused.

Never in my wildest dreams did I think I'd end up with four males who wanted me the way I craved them.

———

LATER THAT DAY, in the vacation rental Grant had procured for us, I was standing under the shower, not wanting to move.

This was the first level of comfort I've had since landing on this island. I ignored the lizards on the ceiling as I lathered my hair with shampoo. Normally, I'd freak out over bugs and such, but I didn't have the energy. My heat was a little more tolerable after mine and Tony's quickie in the closet.

I still craved being around my alphas at all times.

"Are you okay in there?" Wesley called outside the door.

"Yep," I said, rinsing my hair- soap suds all over my wet body. I heard the door open, and I gasped in surprise. "What do you need, Wesley?"

I could see his shadow standing on the other side of the curtain. I felt a little apprehensive and nervous. I wasn't sure what he was going to do.

Then he pulled the curtain open halfway.

I looked at him as I twisted my hair. He stood there, staring at my completely naked body. He wasn't wearing a shirt, just gray sweatpants. I felt a little creeped out but also felt warmth between my legs at his private intrusion.

"Can I wash you?" he asked.

"Um, sure," I said, my heart beating fast. He grabbed the soapy loofah from me. I stood still as he began washing my shoulders, a look of intense concentration in his blue eyes. His caramel-colored hair got wet in the water as he lowered himself, washing my belly next.

"Turn around," he ordered a hint of alpha power in his voice.

The pressure between my legs increased at his command, wanting him to touch me there. I turned around, my inner omega wanting to obey him immediately.

Wesley

MY GOD, she was beautiful.

When wet, her curly black hair stopped at her waist, right above the curve of her buttocks.

I was nervous since she didn't talk to me much as she was too wrapped in Grant's drama earlier today with the Jatix situation. I wanted her to get to know me. Soap and water covered my arms as I pressed the loofah around her glorious butt cheeks one at a time.

The droplets of water made her skin shine. The hardness in my pants made me pause as I pressed her ass harder with the loofah.

I dropped the loofah and rinsed her ass cheeks with my bare hands. She gasped when I squeezed her butt, pulling her cheeks open.

"Do you like washing your women?" she asked me. I could tell she was trying to make light of things, but I could smell her heavy scent of arousal.

"Just you," I said, and it was the truth. Before her, I didn't have these kinds of fantasies. I fantasized about what I'd do with her since I met her on the cruise ship. "Bend over."

I could hear her labored breathing with arousal as she bent down. Her large butt was in the air and dying to be touched. I admired it. Her brown skin glistened under the water, so delectable.

My gaze wandered down, seeing her pussy lips covering the pink rose inside.

"Is that good?" she asked, touching the tub floor with her hands.

"It's perfect," I said in a harsh whisper. I could barely breathe with arousal as I rubbed her ass with my hands, washing the soap off. Her skin was so soft and jiggly. I squeezed her butt cheeks and spread them again. Her pussy lips opened a little, glistening in slick. She was horny for me. I washed between her butt cheeks with my finger, wiping from bottom to top. She stuck her bottom out more, pressing against my finger.

She liked it.

I repeated the motion until I was sure her middle was squeaky clean.

I wanted a taste. I wanted to worship it. She was going to know tonight just how much I loved her bottom.

With one palm on each butt cheek, I spread her open like a feast. I licked around her anal region, pressing my tongue against her ridges. I could hear her moans as I licked her dark hole with my rough, invading tongue, and I loved hearing her moans. I pressed against her little hole, slowly stretching her open. She tried to move away from my invasion, but I gripped her cheeks tight, not allowing her to escape.

"Please don't go inside all the way. It'll hurt," she whimpered.

"I need your tight dark hole, baby," I said. "Open your legs wider for me, sweet thing. I want this after every bath and shower you take."

"Oh," she squeaked in surprise at my request. Her thighs jiggled as she spread them wide for me. Her pussy was hungry for me, judging by how her slick shined down from her pink hole.

She was a gourmet feast waiting for me, and I hadn't even started.

I buried my face between her cheeks, pressing my nose up and down her crack. Smelling every dark inch of her. The place where she hid from the world. Where no one else in the world had gone into. I felt honored that she let me get into her most intimate areas. *Holy,* my cock was so hard, I could feel the pre-cum leaking. I wanted to fuck her tight dark hole, but I didn't want to scare her.

My tongue pressed inside her ass, opening her anal region wider. She gasped at the intrusion, and her butt cheeks clenched around my tongue- fighting me. *Fine*, I'd let her off easy tonight. I instead licked down and spread her pussy lips with my fingers. I lapped up her slick, licking every drop of her honey. I pressed my middle finger inside her pussy, feeling her warmth and slickness. *Delicious.* She moaned as I circled my finger around and around until her legs clenched.

Removing my finger, I brought my finger to her face.

"Taste," I demanded, sticking my finger into her mouth. I could see the surprise in her eyes as her lips closed around it sucking her own juices. The smell of her arousal grew more potent, covering the steamy bathroom.

"Oh, Wesley, you're kinky," she breathed. I went back to licking her pussy. Moving harder and faster until I heard her cry out with her orgasm. As her pussy pulsed with her orgasm, I slid my thick cock inside her. It was the perfect moment. Her pussy clenching my aching cock felt like heaven on earth.

Goddamn.

I stood there on the edge of the bathtub, thrusting my cock deep inside her canal. Her pussy was like a tight vise around my cock, pulling me deeper until I couldn't take it. My cock tensed.

I roared as jets of my semen exploded inside her. I couldn't move as I tried to catch my breath.

"That was fucking amazing," I gasped, helping her stand as my knot filled inside her. I wrapped my hands around her waist, pulling her in tight as we waited for my knot to release her.

Tiana

AFTER OUR MIND-BLOWING SESSION, I cuddled with Wesley on the ginormous bed.

The rest of the pack was out buying food, so I was warm and toasty with Wesley's arms around me. I wore only a bathrobe with nothing underneath. I couldn't forget what he did to me in the bathroom. Even though I was so new in my sexual journey, nothing could top off the heat level of what we just did.

My stomach growled.

"Is my omega hungry?" asked Wesley, chuckling at my obnoxious stomach.

"Hell yes," I muttered, burying my head against his chest. I didn't realize it, but I had wrapped two blankets around me in a circle. Like a freaking nest. I had never done that before, but it was so comforting. I felt at home.

"Don't worry. They're coming soon. Tony texted me."

"Can we talk about what the heck just happened in the shower?" I said. "I never thought you were that freaky."

"God," he said, exhaling. "I couldn't help myself hearing you singing in the shower, Tiana. I'm sorry if it was weird. I know we barely know each other."

"It was the hottest thing to ever happen to me. Like in my entire life," I said in a low voice, and I could see the relief and pride in his eyes.

"Well, that's good to hear," he laughed.

"I want to know more about you," I said, playing with the edge of the fur blanket. "How did you join Grant's pack?"

"As a kid, I had a rough childhood," he said. "Basically, Grant rescued me one day when my mom threw me out of her home. I told him I could go my own way, but Grant wouldn't hear of it. He fed me with what little he had at the time."

"Wow, I'm sorry," I said, feeling a sad ache in my heart for him. My parents were loving, but too overprotective at times. I couldn't imagine living the life he had. I laid my hand on his pale skin, squeezing in comfort. Behind his eyes, I could see the years of torture he had gone through.

"It's okay. It was a long time ago," he said. "Do you miss your family?"

"I do," I said. *But I wasn't ready to go back yet.*

It was amazing exploring feelings that had been repressed all my life. Feelings of lust, desire, and touch.

"I'm sure Grant will take you back to see your parents again. He's a good guy in his heart, even though his decisions can be questionable sometimes," said Wesley.

"How did Grant afford this vacation home?" I asked. I didn't want to talk about going home just yet. I wasn't sure what I wanted to do with my life right now.

I looked around the beautiful and fairly spacious room. It had bright white curtains and a bookshelf. I couldn't wait to get into those books later. The entire house was minimal and covered in white and black furniture.

"He made good money as an undercover cop. When we were stalking...I mean, looking for you."

I heard the door open and heard heavy footsteps entering the house. Grant, Sam, and Tony showed up at the bedroom door holding bowls of shrimp alfredo. My heart lit up with anticipation.

"Food's here," sang Sam.

Eighteen

TIANA

My stomach was no longer spasming every few seconds in pain, and I was able to migrate to the kitchen with the pack. I had already eaten a huge plate of pasta and waited as Grant poured more into my plate. The rest of the men were busy devouring their food.

After all, we had traveled for quite a while on that little boat.

"Ooh, that's enough, I think," I said, smiling as I twirled my fork.

"My baby will eat," said Grant in his gruff voice, which turned me on. I still wasn't sure how I felt about him betraying my trust a few hours earlier, but he was working his way into my heart with food. I stared longingly at the brownies sitting across the table. "Finish your food first, little omega."

"How did you know I wanted those brownies?" I asked indignantly, placing a forkful of creamy pasta into my mouth. It tasted so scrumptious, and I couldn't get enough. Being in heat for so many hours did a number on me.

"I could see how you're staring at it," he chuckled. I was slowly getting full as I ate the last couple of bites.

"That was fast," muttered Wesley, looking at my plate with admiration.

"I think it's my heat. It's making me hungrier than usual," I said, leaning back against my chair and patting my stomach lightly. But I could still eat those brownies, though. I got up from my chair and walked to where Grant sat with the brownies. Before I could reach my hand out for it, he quickly picked me up and set me down on his lap like I weighed nothing at all.

"Hey!" I cried indignantly.

"You'll still get those brownies," said Grant, wrapping one arm around my waist and holding me still. I squirmed over his hardening cock, feeling aroused all over again. He picked up a brownie square and brought it to my mouth. "I want to feed you."

"Oh," I said, and he quickly placed it into my mouth. My mouth closed around the brownie, biting off the corner piece and moaning in delight at how good it tasted.

"Good girl," he said, his voice husky. He seemed to enjoy this way more than I did when his hand around my waist dipped between my legs as I savored the bite.

"More, please."

"Open your mouth, baby. And your legs," he commanded.

I was taken aback by the request, but I quickly obliged. He helped spread my legs until they were hanging outside his knees while his cock twitched against my ass. He fed me another bite of the brownie while he cupped my pussy. The dull ache in my belly had gotten stronger the friskier he was getting with me.

The pain was creeping down to my privates again, making me ache for a knot again.

"I need your knot," I said, my voice muffled with a brownie in my mouth. He squeezed my pussy and nodded, his sideburns brushing against my face causing warm tingles to flow through me.

"Let me take you to the bedroom," he said, picking me up, and I wrapped my legs around his waist, pressing my lips against his neck.

Grant smelled like soap and all alpha.

He headed to the bedroom, slamming the door open with his foot. He dropped me on the bed violently, and I squeaked in surprise, watching him shed his pants quickly. He untied my bathrobe, opening me up like a present on the bed before him.

"Do you like what you see?" I asked, arching my back ever so slightly so my breasts could jut out further.

"I love it. Every inch of you," he said, holding my breasts in his hands and weighing them. "Such luscious tits you got there."

My face heated when he climbed onto the bed next to me, wrapping his hot, wet lips around my right nipple. He made a sucking motion while his tongue rubbed my nipple, sending sparks through my body. I wrapped my hand around his neck, pulling him closer to me. His hand cupped my pussy again, spreading me with two fingers. I held my breath, awaiting his next move. He knew what he wanted, and I didn't have to coach him to do anything.

He rubbed my clitoris, and I bucked against his hand, needing more friction.

"Harder," I moaned, leaning against the pillows as he sucked my breast and played with my clit. He removed his mouth from my breast with a pop and kissed me on the lips instead.

"Like this?" he asked, as his finger went back and forth repeatedly on my clit with added pressure. I felt my orgasm building up. Ready to explode. Ready to cum. But when I was near, he stopped.

"No, don't stop!" I shouted.

"I want you to come when my cock is deep inside you," said Grant with an evil grin. "While my knot is ballooned inside of you."

The thought alone made my pussy clench.

"Fine," I said, feeling slightly sad when his fingers disappeared.

But I wasn't sad anymore when he pushed his large cock inside my pussy, stretching me. He looked down at where we joined.

"Do you see how your pussy stretches around my cock?" he asked, pushing deeper inside of me. "You were made for me, little omega. To take my cock deep inside you."

My eyes rolled back as I enjoyed the sensation of him penetrating me to the fullest.

"I like it," I gasped.

"I'll make you *love* it," he growled, lifting my legs and placing my feet on his shoulders. "Your pussy is hugging my cock so tight in this position."

His manhood pounded into me with every thrust and pull of his cock. He gazed into my eyes and at my bouncing breasts whenever he pulled his hips back and slammed into me. His look of utter possession made me blush. I tried to turn my face away out of shyness, but he reached out, firmly holding my chin to look at him.

"Oh, Grant," I said, breathing hard, unable to take this much closeness.

"I want you to look at me when I make love to you. When I *fuck* you," he growled, holding my gaze. "It's only me and you in this bedroom. Just me and you, sweetheart. Do you feel how hard you made my cock?"

"Yes," I gulped, staring at this beast of an alpha. He was

huge, and I felt so small underneath him when he pounded into me. He grunted with every thrust as he held my gaze. His chest was gleaming with sweat as he rutted into me.

"I'm going to knot inside you, baby," he growled as his cock streamed hot liquid, spilling his seed into me.

My pussy clenched wildly as he quickly rubbed my clit with his fingers between our joined sexes. The rough pad of his thumb rubbed relentlessly until I screamed with my orgasm.

My entire body shuddered and quaked as he held my chin to look at him while he knotted inside me. He was also breathing hard by the time I came down with my pleasure.

"That...that was," I said, unable to form a coherent sentence as I gasped for air. He collapsed next to me, also spent as his knot kept me glued to him.

"Hot as fuck," he said, finishing my sentence. "You are the best thing that ever happened to me."

"How about when you threw me to the other pack?" I whispered, half-joking and also half-serious. I was too scared to trust this man. He could turn on me at any moment. The last time he was knotted inside me, he had betrayed me.

"That's something I will regret for the rest of my life," he replied, grasping my ass and looking at me as he spoke. His gaze was sincere. "It's not something I'm proud of at all. I wish one day you can fully forgive me."

I could feel his sincerity. Without words, I knew. Silently, I kissed him on the lips, and he pulled me to him as he kissed me back.

"Thank you," he said gruffly with droplets of tears in his eyes.

"Are you crying?" I giggled softly, rubbing his tears with my finger.

"Not at all," he said, his mouth quirking into a smile, and I laughed as he kissed me on the mouth again. This time his kiss had a hard greed to it as I felt his tears soak onto my skin.

"I forgive you, Grant," I said.

"I know. I feel it," he muttered against my mouth. "Thank you, Tiana."

Nineteen

TIANA

It had been a week staying at the vacation home on Howl's Edge. I carefully applied eyeshadow on each eyelid, leaning close to the mirror. I was alone in the bedroom dressing up before my big date with the pack, and they were waiting for me downstairs.

I had no idea what Grant had in store for me, but judging from the twinkle in his eye- it made my heart pound with excitement. My face flushed pink as I thought about our crazy morning romp. I still felt every touch. Every kiss and every loving word in my ear. It made me feel like a queen when they treated me like I was the most precious thing in their lives.

Having sex with Grant wasn't like any of the others. He was intense, and it felt like he was claiming me each time, even though he hadn't bitten me yet.

Tony had explained about the mating mark that comes from the leader of the alphas, and I wondered why Grant hadn't claimed me yet. *Was he unsure about our relationship?* My heart hurt at the thought, but I refused to dwell on it.

I applied my pink lip gloss and twirled in front of the tall body mirror. I wore a form-fitting hot pink dress that I picked out from the nearby mall with Wesley and my gold-strapped heels. Of all the guys, Wesley didn't mind shopping with me. In fact, he seemed to enjoy shopping way more than me. I smiled, remembering how excited he got when he saw me in this dress in the fitting room.

I took a deep breath. I was ready to go.

Grabbing my cute gold clutch, I found in one of the marketplaces, I walked out of the room and down the stairs. The murmurs of the men stopped as soon as they sensed my presence at the top of the stairs. My heart began beating hard as I slowly walked down the stairs.

All eyes turned to me.

"Damn," whispered one of the men.

I shyly looked up, seeing all of their gazes glued to me. They all looked mesmerizing in their suits. Sam wore a dark green emerald tie. Grant's look was distinguished in his all-black suit and carefully groomed sideburns with a few gray hairs. His short black hair shined under the light, illuminating his dark eyebrows.

Wesley looked dumbstruck as he gazed at me, and I blushed. He wore a blue tie that matched his eyes.

Tony's hair was slicked back in a shiny man-bun. An aura of intensity and possessiveness hid behind his gaze.

I carefully walked down the last few steps, and Tony quickly made his way to me, holding out his hand.

"Why thank you, sir," I joked as I gracefully placed my hand in his.

He lifted my hand to his lips, kissing it.

"My lady," he growled, playing along.

"You look amazing," said Sam. He was constantly brushing his hair back, and I could tell he was a little nervous. I was still the same person. Just dressed up and not completely naked like how I was all week.

"Thank you, Sam," I said, pulling Tony's hand as I glided

over to Sam, giving him a small peck on the lips. He looked surprised, and his face turned red under the light.

I smiled as we all made our way outside.

There was a beautiful sunset, and I couldn't help but look at the ocean view. The sky was blood orange, and the ocean was calm tonight. The sound of the seagulls calmed my spirits, and I couldn't believe how much I fell in love with Howl's Edge. It was a quiet island in general. They had their bad side of the island, with all the auctions. But this side of the island, the south side, was full of life, wonder, and excitement.

A large carriage waited outside. My heart almost burst with excitement at the sight of it. They did this for me?!

There were even real horses in the front with a driver.

"Do you like it?" asked Grant.

"I can't believe this," I said, flabbergasted.

Grant hopped up steps and held his hand out for me. I released Tony and grasped Grant's hand as I climbed up the little steps. I sat between Grant and Tony as the carriage started moving.

"How the hell you afford all this, Grant?" asked Sam as they all crowded into the carriage.

"New business ventures," said Grant vaguely. "You're pretty quiet, Tiana. Is everything okay?"

"Yes, I'm just admiring everything," I said. I was enjoying the feel of the air on my face and hair. And how beautiful the palm trees looked from up here and the majestic black horses. "Thank you so much. It's so romantic."

Grant leaned down and kissed me on the forehead. That kiss felt more intimate than even a kiss on the lips. Like he treasured me.

"I'm glad you like it," he whispered.

"Where are we going?" I asked.

"To a restaurant called The Savory Rose."

"Ooh, mister fancy pants," I teased. He chuckled. As we

passed by the island people, they would stop and stare at me. The new omega in town. And her alphas surrounding her protectively. My heart warmed, but I also wondered why Grant hadn't felt the need to mark me as theirs.

"You look a little sad," said Tony, who seemed to be quietly observing me. Grant quickly looked back at me.

My face heated as I wondered how I would say it. Would it make me sound too needy and attached? Maybe Grant didn't see me as forever material yet?

I wasn't sure.

"It's just...how come you haven't marked me yet?" I asked. "Are you all waiting to see if I'm the perfect omega for you?"

I was watching Grant's face. A pained expression came over his face, and he closed his eyes. Then he opened his eyes and held my gaze. He held my trembling hands and pulled them onto his lap.

"I absolutely want to fucking mark you. I want to claim you as mine. Ours," he said, enunciating each word carefully.

My chest rose and fell faster with each breath.

"Then why haven't you?" I said in a low voice.

He rubbed his thumbs over my hands in circles. "I want to make sure you're ready. That you want us despite us taking you from your home."

"But will I ever see my family?" I pressed.

He stayed quiet, and I grew worried. I fidgeted in my seat, wanting space from him. He sensed that as he leaned down to kiss my neck. His warm lips pressed on my neck, causing spirals of warmth to go through me. He lightly grazed my neck with his teeth, and an electricity of lust shot through me. I could feel the wetness gather immediately between my legs as I gave in and dropped my head to one side.

Giving him access.

He kissed me again, and I moaned under his touch.

"You smell so good," he whispered in my ear.

"Oh, Grant," I blushed, pushing him away. I could feel the heat from the other guys' gaze.

"When you say the word, we'll visit your family. It's up to you," Grant finally replied. "I can't keep you hostage here."

I nodded. I wasn't sure if I was ready to see them yet, but I just needed the reassurance.

"Looks like we're here," said Tony to my right, grasping my hand. I looked back at Grant and smiled apologetically as I held Tony's hand to the restaurant. Grant looked a little annoyed, but he held it in. These men were low-key jealous if I showed one person more affection than the other. I didn't understand why they were jealous when it was normal for alphas to share.

Sometimes, I felt like I was the problem. The one causing tension between them.

But I forgot all that as we walked into the restaurant. I gasped at how pretty it was. It was lit in purple from floor to ceiling. The chandeliers were stunning and massive. There were round tables everywhere with purple chairs, and some had one royal red chair in the middle.

"An omega-alpha table for you, sir?" asked a waiter.

"Yes," replied Grant.

We were led to one of the tables, and Sam pulled the red chair for me.

"Thank you, Sam," I said.

"This is the omega throne," he said lavishly, presenting the chair for me. I laughed and sat on the extra cushioned seat. It felt amazing being treated like royalty.

The waiter then took our orders, and I sipped on water while waiting for my food to arrive. My stomach growled, and I was extra hungry for some reason. Maybe it was the constant sexual romps I had with the men.

"How do you like this place?" asked Wesley, his blue eyes trained on me.

"It's so beautiful," I said.

"Beautiful like you," said Tony, who was sitting next to me, touching my thigh.

———

Tony

SEEING Grant kiss Tiana like that pissed me off. I knew it was irrational, but I was still annoyed. This date was supposed to be for Tiana and us as a group.

But Grant was making it all about him. I could see the other guys were feeling tense at the connection Grant was making with her. I barely had any time with her. Every guy was fighting for her attention.

Tiana was so pretty, sitting in her special omega chair, looking small on her throne. Her pink lips looked soft and kissable. I couldn't help but touch her thigh underneath the table. Her face was turning a beautiful shade of pink at my touch. She tried moving her thigh away, but I held it in place under my hand. She wasn't going anywhere.

My dick hardened under my suit pants. This wasn't the best place to be aroused.

But I couldn't help it.

"I would like to get to know your past a little better. Did you guys enjoy your careers before coming back to Howl's Edge?" she asked the group at large. "Except for you, Sam, of course. The pirate man."

"The pirate man?" laughed Sam, shaking his head.

"Well, you dress like one most of the time, and you love being out at sea," said Tiana.

"You have a point there," Sam smiled.

"I loved being a cop," said Grant. "How about you, Wes?"

"It led us to Tiana. That's all that matters," said Wesley. "But I did enjoy it from time to time."

Then Tiana looked over at me.

"Not me," I said. "I'd rather create my music all day."

"Wait, do you play?" she asked in surprise, her attention on me.

"Yep, I play guitar," I said. Her gaze always threw me off guard. When she turned her full attention on me, the nervousness in my stomach intensified. Ever since I introduced myself to her on the cruise, my head wasn't right. I hadn't even focused enough to play the guitar.

Our steaks arrived. Mine was a large tomahawk steak, and I looked over at Tiana eating her filet. She was eating with gusto, and that made me even hornier. I imagined her mouth wrapped around my cock, where it should be.

This little woman could eat. And I loved it.

"Mhm, that was so good," she said after cleaning her plate.

I ate one more bite of the steak, not really focusing on it. I wanted her.

"Do you need to use the bathroom? I can take you there," I offered.

"Yes, thank you, Tony."

I could feel the other men's suspicious gazes.

"Don't be getting ideas there, man," said Sam, scratching his head nervously. I winked at him, and he shook his head.

I took Tiana's hand, leading her toward the other side of the building. Following the signs- we passed by tables of alphas and omegas. The bathrooms were secluded in the corner of the restaurant. We turned the corner, and I pulled her up against the wall.

"I already know what you want," she said quietly. I could hear the clinking of plates, forks, and people chattering away in the dining area. My heart stopped when she said that. She was perceptive with those innocent doe eyes.

"Good," I said, growling low in her ear. She shivered, and I captured her lips with mine. Kissing her deep.

I looked for a private area and saw a room next to the bathroom marked Alpha Omega Privacy Room. Damn, this restaurant thought of everything. No wonder it was highly rated. We were coming back here again.

We went into the room, and I quickly locked the door. It was a small room complete with a fancy bed in the middle.

She threw her arms around me, kissing me hard. I smelled her scent of arousal and her eagerness. She was just as horny for me as I was for her.

"Are you the type of guy who likes quickies?" she asked breathlessly against my neck as she lifted her lips from mine.

I instantly remembered the quickie we had in the broom closet.

"Maybe it just turns me on," I whispered, lifting her tight-ass dress over her luscious butt. I squeezed each butt cheek, feeling the globe of them in my palms. It was the most amazing feeling in the world. She played with my cock, wrapping her fingers around it from outside my pants.

I felt all the blood rush there, my cock hardening even more.

"Let me take care of you," she said, and I quickly unbuckled my pants. She pulled my cock out of my boxers. It needed attention, and I couldn't believe what she was about to do.

I stood over her as she went down on her knees. She hesitantly touched my penis like it was some foreign object. She squeezed and played with my cock, getting acclimated to it.

She licked the tip of my cock. Ever so slowly. Fuck.

Her teasing was torturous.

"I thought you were a virgin?" I gasped.

"It's not like I never watched x-rated videos," she winked from below. God, my scrotum immediately tightened.

She continued licking my cock slowly from the bottom to the top. She licked my precum carefully and slowly, sticking her tongue out longer than necessary so I could see the white precum on her pink tongue.

"You're torturing me, baby. I'm about to spread you open on that dirty bed," I threatened.

"Patience, big boy," she breathed on my cock. I groaned, feeling her hot breath on my dick. Her antics were turning me on even more. Then she pulled my cock into her mouth. It was too big for her, so only half of me entered her mouth. I felt the warm tightness of her lips, mouth, and throat.

Going up and down.

Licking around and around like a popsicle.

I grabbed the sides of the counter as my knees buckled. She looked up at me with those big eyes, her head bobbing up and down. My cock was warm and wet in her mouth. I couldn't take it anymore. My balls tightened, and I exploded in her mouth.

She was taken by surprise as she quickly tried to swallow, but it was too much as it spilled over her chin.

"Damn," I gasped as soon as I regained my breath. She was thoroughly trying to clean my cock with her tongue. Every last drop. "Please, no. You're our queen, baby."

"I want to," she rasped. "When I'm horny and off the pills-it's completely different. I want to do all the dirty, filthiest things you can think of."

Fuck.

Licking off the remaining cum from my cock, she stood up and washed up in the little sink, and touched up her hair.

As I watched her, I remembered my late father lecturing me about alpha-hood. About omegas and how important she is to a pack. That I needed to treat my future omega as a queen.

"An omega is like a jewel to a pack," I said out loud.

"Oh, what?" she asked, applying lipstick after cleaning up.

"You're like a jewel to us, Tiana," I said. "If anyone ever disrespects you, they'll answer to me."

"Is it because of good sex?" joked Tiana.

"Tiana, I'm being serious," I said. She liked to joke when she was nervous. I was starting to learn that about her. "If anyone ever disrespects you, I'll come for him."

I could tell she was taken aback by the seriousness of my statement.

"Okay," she said, taking my hand. "Come on, let's go back. I'm sure the others are wondering what we're doing."

I grinned.

"Let them wonder," I replied.

Twenty

TIANA

After dinner at *The Savory Rose*, the carriage ride back to the house felt tense between the males. When we reached the front door, and I got off the carriage, the men started fighting behind me.

Oh no.

I turned back to see what was happening.

"She was trying to enjoy a nice dinner before you took her away," Grant growled.

"And you didn't need to steal all her attention during the ride there," said Tony. "I have every right to her as you do. I don't think you understand that, Grant."

I could see Grant's hackles rise at Tony's disrespect.

"Stop!" I shouted. "You're all acting immature."

"It's easy for you to say. You'll never understand how you affect us alphas," Tony said.

I blinked in shock. *What the hell?*

"You know what? I'm done," I said, turning on my heel. "I'm going to my room. I don't want to see anyone tonight."

I stalked off into the dark house and up the stairs, my heels clicking on the marble flooring.

I couldn't believe it. I never asked to be here. I never asked to be shared by all these alphas. I didn't give a shit about anything anymore, and everything in my life happened way too fast.

Every step I took up the stairs felt like a jab to my own heart.

I passed by the men's bedrooms and went into the master bedroom, which was my room. Locking the door behind me, I switched the light on and threw myself on the bed.

I lay on my side, thinking of what I needed to do. I needed to go home. Ever since I arrived, the pack wasn't the same. They'd be better off without me.

Pain stabbed in my chest. I had never felt like this before.

It was like a physical pain to the heartbreak I felt at the thought of leaving the Frostcrown Pack. I would be alone again in a world of humans who didn't understand me. But it was okay. I would be strong and one day find my true mates.

I cried in bed, streaks of black mascara smeared all over the white pillows.

I didn't think I could form such strong connections in so little time. I was going to miss Tony's attentive care for my emotions. Wesley's admiration of my bottom. Grant's possessive way he took my body and Sam's lightheartedness and care. I was going to miss all of that.

After crying my heart out, I got off the bed and began to gather my things in the closet.

Maybe it was time to go back home.

I had a few pajamas, dresses, and a phone they bought for me, but that was it. I sat on the closet floor, leaning against the dresses. If I decided this wasn't for me, it wouldn't take much time to pack everything and go.

There was a soft knock on the door. I sniffed and sat on the floor, staring at the bottom of my heels. I didn't feel like talking to anyone.

"Tiana?" said Sam's voice. He sounded nervous but also gentle. "Tiana, I know you can hear me in there. Please open the door. I just want to talk."

A pang went through my heart, hearing his voice.

"I'm not ready," I called out. My body was heavy with sadness, and I couldn't get up off the floor. I didn't want to do it anymore. The way Tony spoke to me was so dismissive and disrespectful.

"Tiana," said Sam again, this time lowering his voice and using the alpha baritone in his voice. My inner omega wolf wanted to obey him, and my chest hurt even more as I tried to fight it. "No one blames you for anything. I promise."

Tears threatened to fall again. Biting my lip, I slowly shuffled to the door and unlocked it.

Sam opened the door, and upon seeing my face, he wiped the tears from my cheeks with his callused thumbs.

He pulled me in for a hug.

As I leaned into him, he smelled like candle wax and honey. He was like a warm bear, which felt comforting and instantly made me feel more at ease.

"I'm sorry they were acting like asses," he said, his voice muffled against my hair. I turned and kissed him on the mouth, my lips brushing against his small mustache.

He placed both hands on either side of my face and captured my lips with his. My eyes closed, taking in the feelings. His alpha scent was seductive and full of possibilities. His tongue claimed my mouth, and I mewled softly under his dominance. He groaned and pressed his body up against me. His erection was evident.

"I want you right now," he said, and I opened my eyes. He rubbed his hands down my body, over my tight pink dress. His hands roamed my thighs underneath. "All day, I've wanted you. Wanting to fuck you so bad."

"You were my first," I whispered as he laid me on the soft

bed. The white blankets were messy from all my crying. The drapes were still open, showing the fiery sunset outside.

"Exactly, and I don't intend to have you forget that," he said, lifting my dress above my waist and exposing my pink panties. He kissed my thighs, his body heat making me shiver in anticipation. I wanted his lips against my core. "Your panties are drenched with slick, baby."

Moving my panties to the side, he touched me with one finger, sliding it from the bottom to the top, teasing my clitoris.

"Sam," I groaned, the back of my head pressing against the pillow in my arousal. I was so turned on that I wanted more. "I need you inside me."

I started pulling down my panties, but he swiftly took charge, ripping them off me. Then he unbuckled his belt, and heat spiraled in my pussy. He threw his slacks to the floor of the bed and was on top of me again. The body heat emanating from his alpha body was tempting. I touched his chest and felt his biceps. His mouth turned up in a half-smile at my exploration.

"Do you like it?"

"I do," I breathed.

"Are you ready for me, baby? I don't want to rush you," he said, kissing my boobs. His hot breath made my nipples hard, and I nodded. He quickly spread my legs with his knee, and his hand cupped my sex. "Your pussy is dripping in my hand."

"I'm hot for you, Sam."

He stuck a finger inside me, and I moaned. He teased me with his finger as he slowly went in and out.

"How is that?" he asked.

"I need something bigger," I said, feeling shy talking like this. But this was turning me on like crazy. My pussy was clenching and tightening around his middle finger, wanting more. I was starting to realize that Sam prolonged foreplay more than any of the men here. He seemed to be enjoying this.

"Do you want my dick inside you?" he said, placing a second finger inside me, stretching me. My heart raced, and my breasts swelled. Removing his fingers, he licked them one by one while looking me in the eyes. He was a man of deep passion, and I felt like the only one for him right now. "You taste so good, princess."

"I want you," I begged, spreading my legs wider. He reveled at the display, his eyes glued to my sex. Then, in one swift motion, he mounted me and pushed inside me with a groan while his eyes closed in pleasure.

My pussy stretched wide around his invading dick as he pushed deeper and deeper.

We locked eyes as our sexes joined, and he was fully inside me now. He rocked his hips, thrusting into me. I tightened my legs around him in blissful pleasure, taking him in. Feeling his rock-hard cock inside me, sturdy and hot.

"Your pussy is glorious. My beautiful female," he breathed as he rocked faster and faster. "Tighter, baby."

I clenched my pussy tight around his thrusting cock as he humped against me. My pussy walls contracted as waves of pleasure went through every inch of my body.

"Harder, Sam," I gasped.

He bucked his hips with more intensity into me, and his sack slapped against my ass, heightening the feeling.

With every thrust and rub against my clit, I arched higher, and I finally convulsed underneath him. A crescendo of fireworks exploded through my body as I came. Moaning his name.

He thrust one final time, roaring as he orgasmed.

"Fuck," he howled, kissing me hard on the mouth.

His ejaculate spewed inside me, some of it seeping out as his dick hardened and knotted inside me. Swelling and stretching me open in pleasurable glory. He lay on top of me as we tried to catch our breath.

"That was fucking amazing," I said, and Sam chuckled. "What's so funny?"

"I never heard you swear before," he muttered against my neck as his finger traced my belly. "I don't think I'm a good influence. Maybe you should go to a better-behaved pack."

"Oh, shut up," I said, tensing up.

Sam seemed to sense my mood.

"Sorry, I guess it's too soon to joke about that," he said, pulling me in tight for a cuddle.

"I know you're joking," I sighed. "Sometimes, I have nightmares about it—the thought of being helpless for that one moment, thinking I lost everything."

"I'm sorry," said Sam. "Sometimes I wish I stood up more that day. The first day when we gave you to the Lustfur Pack."

"I don't blame you, Sam," I said quickly, turning on my side to face him. I rubbed his muscular forearm, covered in black hair. "I don't blame anyone anymore."

Sam kissed me softly. His knot was beginning to go down.

"The pack is waiting for us," he said. "Are you ready to see them now?"

"I am," I said, feeling much better after Sam's lightheartedness and the mind-blowing sex we just had.

After getting cleaned up in the bathroom, I met Sam back in the bedroom, his pants on and belt buckled.

We walked out of the backdoor, and I saw rose petals all over the ground, leading into a trail to the backyard. I gasped at the sight ahead of us.

"What's going on?" I asked. My nose was still stuffy from all my crying. There were strings of little lights surrounding the backyard, illuminating the night.

Tony was sitting in a chair in the middle of the backyard,

holding a guitar across his lap. Grant and Wesley stood on either side of him. Wesley smiled hugely upon seeing me.

Tony started playing the guitar, and Sam hurried to bring me a chair. At first, I was confused, but then my heart began to warm as he played the guitar and sang a song for me.

Tears sprang to my eyes that they would do all this for me.

"Ever since you came into our lives, Miss Tiana.

You lit our world and knocked off Sam's bandana.

More than you ever know. More than we ever dreamt.

You belong with our pack. Make no mistake.

So tonight we have a special question..."

I didn't know what to feel. I was overwhelmed and also touched. I couldn't believe Tony wrote a song just for me.

My heart was beating fast as Grant walked over to me. I tried to stand, but Sam gently sat me down. *What was happening?*

"Tiana, I'm sorry for the way we spoke to you. Please forgive us," Grant said, then he knelt, holding a box out in his hand. "I want to mark you and claim you as ours. I know this is fast, but I'm falling for you, Tiana. Can you forgive me?"

I thought about it for a moment. His eyes conveyed honesty, and his gaze was powerful. My inner omega energy desperately wanted peace with this alpha male.

"Yes," I said softly, my heart nearly bursting.

Then he popped the box open, and I gasped. It was a large diamond ring with four stones.

"Each stone symbolizes each of us," he said. "Will you be ours after tonight? For me to mark you and claim you?"

I was scared of what that meant. They had told me that when a pack claimed an omega, it was commitment forever. After the actual marking happens, the omega would desire to do whatever the alphas wanted to make him happy, and vice versa.

I would be theirs forever. But I knew I didn't want to be separated from them.

I loved them all.

"Yes," I whispered, laughing and crying as he slid the ring onto my finger. It felt heavy on my hand, and it felt so good. Grant kissed me on the lips, and I kissed him back, feeling the light wind in my hair.

"Have you all forgiven each other?" I asked when we pulled apart.

"We have come to an agreement," said Grant.

"And what's that?"

"We will take nightly turns with you, so each alpha gets a fair amount of intimacy with you. Then once a week, it'll be all of us in one night," he said. "If you want a night just for yourself, I'll make it happen too. Not that we'll be too happy about that."

"It sounds nice," I said. They had it figured out, and it would be fair. I liked the idea, which would allow me to bond with each of them.

"We'll start the first week with your pick for the night, and then we rotate," said Tony.

"Who's it going to be for tonight?" asked Grant.

"All of you," I said to the shock of them all.

I squealed when Grant lifted me off my chair.

We kissed under the moonlight as he grabbed me and twirled around in circles in the backyard. He released me, and Wesley kissed me on the lips next. His kiss was eager and soft, making my heart flutter like a teenager in love.

Sam turned me towards him and dipped my body as he kissed me after. It was intense with Sam, and I could feel the heat of desire bridle from him again, making my body respond right away to him, wetness gathering in my core.

Then Tony grabbed me next, and our kiss was deep and

sensual as he placed his hand behind my neck, pulling me in towards him.

I wanted them all tonight, and I couldn't wait.

Twenty-One

GRANT

I was going to mark her tonight.

Tiana agreed to be ours, and I couldn't believe it. We were in the master bedroom- in her room and sanctuary.

I was feasting between her legs on the bed. She was a glorious beauty spread out for us, naked except for her heels and jewelry.

All our suits lay scattered across the bed and the floor, forgotten as we focused on our omega. Wesley played with her ass while Sam and Tony toyed with her breasts, sucking her nipples.

I had the coveted spot. Right where I wanted to be.

"Such a good little omega," said Tony, and she blushed.

Slick covered her pussy as I licked her, sliding my tongue between her folds and her swollen clitoris.

She tried to close her legs in shyness. Tiana was still shy anytime I got too close like that.

"Open up, Tiana," I growled.

I purred against her pussy to calm her, and she slowly widened her legs again. The vibration from my purr got her off every time, and I knew she enjoyed it.

Wesley's fingers were rubbing her anus, feeling her out. I watched as he placed a finger coated with saliva inside her tight entrance.

She gasped, and my dick hardened at the sight.

I turned back to her pussy, licking her honey as she moaned. Her clit was engorged and pink. I flicked my tongue over it, sucking her tiny bud. She moaned in pleasure, grabbing my hair.

Fuck, she smelled so good. Her musky strawberry omega scent made my heart pound even faster. I wanted to lick every inch of her.

I probed into her pussy with my tongue. Fucking her with my tongue, she arched her hips towards me, opening up for me wider.

"Damn," said Wesley. "She's open wide for you, man."

"Mhmm," I said, my voice muffled against her pussy. I pressed my tongue deeper inside her, tasting her delicious strawberry essence. Then I circled her clitoris with my tongue, pressing on the little pink nub while I fingered her.

"More," she begged feverishly. I quickly placed another finger inside her, and she moaned loudly. I pumped into her and saw that Wesley had stuck a second finger inside her ass.

She didn't flinch. She widened her legs further apart. Her skin was bronze under the moonlight coming in from the open window.

She looked exquisite.

I licked her harder and faster until she started to tremble. I knew she was close.

"I'm going to penetrate you, sweetheart," I said, sitting up on my knees. I rubbed the tip of my dick at her entrance, preparing her and covering my member with her slick. My heart beat faster with excitement. I couldn't wait for her pussy to hug my dick, to cling to her alpha while I rut her.

As I pressed inside her heated slit- I watched her pretty face, her eyes closing in pleasure.

"Do you like that, little omega?" I asked her.

"Oh god, yes," she replied as we locked eyes. It was a completely different feeling this time, serving to harden my cock even further.

"Tiana, I'm going to take you from behind," said Wesley. "My cock is going inside your ass."

"No, please," whined Tiana, her eyes fluttering open. "It's going to hurt."

"If it hurts, I'll stop," said Wesley.

I carried her off the bed, and she clung to my neck, my dick still nestled inside her pussy.

I kept her legs spread around my waist while Wesley went around to take her ass.

***

Tiana

MY HEART WAS BEATING FAST in arousal and fear.

Having a large overgrown cock inside me was one thing... but to have another attempt to go into my ass was something else. Wesley spread my cheeks, and I bit into Grant's arm as Wesley placed the tip of his cock inside my ass.

I heard him spit on his cock behind me, lubing it up, and fear went through me.

It stung as he slowly inserted his cock inside me, and I cried out. Stretching my ass to the limit as he pushed in, inch by inch.

"Tell me to stop if it hurts," said Wesley.

"No, I can handle it," I whimpered. I wanted to feel all of it as an omega. I yelped in shock as he slowly thrust his entire cock inside of me, stretching me.

"Shh," purred Wesley in my ear. "Your virgin ass feels so good."

I felt both of them thrusting into me. I felt like a rag doll in the middle as my breasts bounced up and down.

Both cocks were pulsing and thrusting into me simultaneously, overwhelming me with sensation. I saw Tony on the bed, lazily pumping his penis with his hand as he watched my breasts bounce. Sam was watching the show as well, his cock hard in his hand.

It aroused me that they were watching—my slick increasing between my legs.

I turned back to Grant, and he captured my lips in a deep kiss. His tongue probed my mouth, and I closed my eyes. Our tongues swirled around each other. Both cocks inside me felt so good and made me feel so full.

Something that I had been craving but never knew.

Grant's teeth grazed my collarbone, and I held my breath.

Was he going to mark me? In the middle of his rut?

His teeth punctured my skin, and I whimpered. The pain was burning hot at first. Then, he licked my neck, growling in my ear in a very intimate display of possessiveness. The pain instantly cooled off.

"Ours forever," he said, his hot breath grazing my ear, marking me.

My pussy clenched tight with excitement, feeling the burn of his bite down to my belly. Wetness gushed from me, and I screamed from my instant orgasm. My body shook from my climax as they pumped furiously inside me.

Grant roared as he came, kissing my neck all the while. Wesley kissed the back of my neck, biting me as he exploded inside my ass.

And both of them knotted inside me, stretching me to the limit.

After Grant had marked me, my privates were more open

and able to receive them more easily. It was as if my body magically knew that I was made for this pack.

Grant and Wesley carried me to the bed, laying me in the middle. Wesley spooned me from behind, and Grant was in front.

Kisses rained down on my skin from every man in the room.

Tony was kissing my thighs, and Sam began kissing my breasts. The room smelled like sweat, masculine energy, and my strawberry scent. Every man in here was mine. I leaned over to Grant's neck, licking him. Then I nipped him, drawing blood.

"You're mine," I said, and his eyes widened in surprise. He kissed me on the lips, licking the blood away.

"I love you, Tiana," said Grant.

"I love you too," I said, and his eyes glowed with excitement.

"I'm glad we found you and that I took on the mission so long ago," said Grant.

"Me too," I whispered against his lips.

I turned towards Wesley and marked him, biting him on the shoulder.

"Where I wanted it," he whispered. Then he looked at the little bite proudly. "Claimed by an omega."

"Sam," I said. And he lowered his neck to my mouth. I licked the spot I wanted and bit him with a savage urge. I needed to claim him. All of them. Sam embraced and kissed me passionately while Grant and Wesley were still inside me.

"Tony next," I said.

Sam moved out of the way, and Tony kissed my mouth before I marked him.

"I love you," said Tony. My heart grew in size at his words. As each of them professed his love for me, I felt my core heating up again.

"I love you all," I whispered.

And so the night continued with more lovemaking, and I basked in their attention.

The next morning, I yawned and stretched.

Wesley and Sam were still sleeping on either side of me. Grant and Tony were off to work. They were off to work at a watch company for an alpha named Caleb.

I slowly removed Sam's arm from my chest and Wesley's hand on my butt as I slithered off the bed, trying not to wake them. When I stood up, I suddenly felt dizzy and had to grab the nightstand.

I felt sick to my stomach and had the urge to throw up.

Quickly running to the bathroom, I vomited into the toilet.

"Oh no, Tiana," said Wesley, coming up behind me. He grabbed a tissue and wiped my mouth when I was done. I was breathing hard by the time I was done, and I still didn't feel right. The dizziness nearly clouded my vision.

"I feel dizzy," I said.

"Wait, that normally happens to pregnant omegas," he observed, touching my face. "Oh."

My stomach sank with instant worry.

Sam came running into the bathroom wearing a towel around his waist.

"Is everything okay in here?" he asked, his face shocked as he saw me kneeling in front of the toilet.

"She threw up," said Wesley. Sam knelt next to me, touching my forehead and feeling for a fever. "I think she needs a pregnancy test."

"A what?!" exclaimed Sam. "Already?"

"I don't think I'm pregnant," I said vehemently. I was too young, and I still hadn't figured out my life.

"I'll go buy the pregnancy test," said Sam, flustered as he ran out of the bathroom. "Wesley, you stay and watch her."

"I will," said Wesley.

I slowly got up and, with Wesley's help, walked back to the bed. I heard the front door slam as Sam rushed out to buy a pregnancy test.

"Do you want a baby?" I asked.

"We all do," said Wesley. "An alpha's job is to procreate, so this will bring joy to us all and the island. Each birth is announced and celebrated. Why aren't you excited, Tiana?"

"I just don't know what I'm doing with my life right now," I said, panicking. "I don't think I'm ready."

I imagined holding a little baby and taking care of them.

It sounded too scary to think about right now. The enormity of the responsibility I was going to have was overwhelming. And we just claimed each other last night. I was freshly mated to this pack.

After the dizziness passed, I brushed my teeth with Wesley standing protectively behind me in case I fell, even though I reassured him constantly that I was feeling a little better. Wesley helped wash me in the shower without doing any of the sensual stuff he usually did to me. He was treating me gently, and I was grateful. My stomach hurt from time to time.

Hearing the front door open, I quickly turned off the water, and Wesley grabbed a towel, wrapping it around me.

"I have the pregnancy test!" shouted Sam as he came up the stairs. He came into the bathroom, holding the pink box in his hand.

"I feel a little better now," I said. "Do I really need to take it?"

"Yes," said Wesley, opening the package for me. "We'll wait outside the door."

WE SAT ON THE BED, waiting for the timer to go off, as the pregnancy test sat on the bathroom counter.

The bathrobe I wore didn't stop the chills from going through me. I was feeling cold and panicky. What would my parents think? Well they encouraged this to happen anyway...

Sam wrapped his arm around me. His arm was large and warm.

"If she's pregnant, do you want a boy or a girl?" Sam asked Wesley.

"I wouldn't mind either, but an alpha would be a nice addition to our family," said Wesley.

I rolled my eyes. They sounded a little too excited at the prospect. I didn't think I was pregnant. It was probably the steak from last night not sitting well with me. Just a little food poisoning, that's all.

I stared at the timer on Sam's phone as he held it between us.

It was getting closer—one more minute.

My breathing accelerated as I watched the timer. Three. Two. One.

"It's time," said Sam.

I walked to the bathroom, the men following behind me. Lifting the test, I stared at the word displayed on the screen:

Pregnant

"Oh my god," I said, holding my mouth in shock.

"What does it say?" asked Wesley breathlessly. I held the test up toward them. Straight away, big smiles came across their faces. I was in pure shock. I know I shouldn't be in shock since I did nothing to prevent it, but I didn't think it could happen this fast.

Dizziness blurred my vision again, and I held the counter for balance. Wesley rushed over to me, holding my arm.

"We're going to have a baby," said Sam, a dreamy look coming over his face.

"I'm not feeling so well," I said. "Need to go back to bed."

We walked out of the bathroom with Wesley and Sam on either side of me, helping me get back to bed.

"Grant is going to be over the moon," said Wesley. "Tiana, I'm sorry you're not feeling well, and you have to be the one to suffer. But in the end, it'll be amazing!"

"Thanks for your comforting words," I said, smiling through my dizziness. I imagined holding a tiny baby in my arms, my tummy round with pregnancy. Laying on the bed, Sam tucked me into the blankets.

"I'll make you ginger tea," said Wesley, leaving the room with a bounce to his step.

A little bit of excitement was starting to course through me. And also fear.

As my head cleared, I looked at Sam as he was scrolling through his phone with his other hand around me. His face had a glow to it.

"I'm booking an appointment for you at the Omega Birthing Center," he said.

"There's a specific hospital for omegas?" I asked. "How come?"

"Omegas are built differently with wider hips to carry alpha babies," he said. "If there is an emergency, a hospital catered to omegas is the best option."

"I have to tell my parents about this," I said, starting to panic. "We need to fly to Seattle as soon as possible."

"Are you freaking out, Tiana?" said Sam, setting his phone down.

"Just a little," I whined, laying on his chest for comfort. He began purring softly with his body, its vibrations calming my racing heart.

"Tell Grant tonight and see what he says," said Sam. "If he flips out, I'll beat him up for you."

I giggled.

"Do you think he'll get upset that I want to see my family?" I asked, and my stomach somersaulted with nervousness at the thought.

"Na, I don't think so," said Sam, rubbing my stomach. "I can't wait until you start to swell with our baby in you. You're going to look so hot."

I laughed. "You're so bad, Sam."

"It's true, baby," he grinned, leaning down to kiss me. As I drank my ginger tea that day, I was excited as we talked about the baby.

But the dread of confronting Grant to take me to my family loomed over me.

Twenty-Two

GRANT

I munched on popcorn, preparing to watch a movie of my pack's choice.

We sat as a family in the living room, Tiana sitting next to me on the couch.

I noticed that there was something off about Tiana tonight. She refused to eat any of the popcorn even though she usually devoured my bucket before I even got a chance. Her face looked tired, and I was starting to be concerned.

"Tiana, you normally love popcorn. What's going on?" I asked.

She turned to me, biting her lip. There was something on her mind. Her beautiful face conveyed nervousness. Why was she so scared?

"Grant, I have something to tell you," she said. "Tony, you'll want to hear this too."

"What is it?" I asked, concerned. This was serious, judging by the look on her face.

"We're having a baby," she said.

What?! An indescribable feeling of happiness coursed

through my entire being. My alpha wolf rejoiced at success-fully mating this woman.

"I can't believe it," said Tony.

Tears came to my eyes. "I'm so fucking happy."

Hugging her and feeling her soft warmth against my body felt incredible as I pulled her in. We all hugged, laughed, and shared in our joy of bringing a baby into the family. I was more than ready to be a father.

It was about damn time.

"I'm glad you're not upset," she said breathlessly from all our hugs on the couch.

"Why in the world would you think that?" I asked, kissing her forehead and touching her hair.

"Because you're so big and scary," she whispered, and my cock hardened at her words. "But there's something else too."

"Oh?"

"I want to see my family as soon as possible," she said, biting her lower lip. Fuck, when she bit her lip like that...

I hesitated at her request. She was right, though. Her family needed to know. It wasn't like the old times when kidnapping omegas was okay and didn't have to tell anyone.

"We'll go tomorrow morning then if you're feeling up to it," I said quickly when her face fell at my hesitance.

"She's been having morning sickness," said Wesley, and Tiana rolled her eyes.

"Tiana, we can't have you running around if you're feeling sick," I said.

"Please, Grant! It's just going to get worse the longer I sit around," said Tiana, her face flushing pink with annoyance. "Just keep bringing me ginger tea and apples. I'll be fine."

"Apples, huh?" I said. "Fine, I'll get in contact with my business partner, Caleb. He has a private jet."

"Thank you so much," said Tiana, putting her soft lips over mine.

"Anything for you," I mumbled against her lips, taking in her essence and her warm, feminine body.

***

Tiana

MY HEART WAS BEATING a mile a minute.

We were standing in front of my parents' apartment door, and I was suddenly unsure if I should knock or not. I couldn't bring my hand up to knock. I called Lori as soon as our plane landed. It was such a relief. I cried on our way here in the taxi. It felt like old times, and it felt amazing to talk to her again. I told her I was traveling with family when she insisted on seeing me.

"Are you going to knock?" asked Grant in his deep voice.

I sighed and knocked three times.

"Who is it?" called Dad soon after, his heavy footsteps shuffling to the door. I heard the clanging of the chain as he was unlocking it.

"It's Tiana."

The door opened immediately, and my dad came hurling through, crushing me in the biggest hug. I hugged him back. A feeling of warmth and safety rushed over me, and tears blurred my vision. I didn't realize how much I missed him.

"You're alive," he said, his breath coming out in gasps. He pulled away and grabbed my face in his hands to look at me. Inspecting my face.

"I'm alive, Dad," I reassured him, instantly regretting not speaking to them earlier from the devastated look on his face. I couldn't call them when I was on Howl's Edge since their government blocked contact with anyone outside the werewolf island.

Then, he noticed the men standing around the door.

"This must be them," he began.

"Who is that?" called my mom from the kitchen.

"This is my alpha pack," I told him. Dad's eyes widened, even though I remembered him clearly telling me to mate the pack.

"Oh, your mom isn't going to be happy," he said. Then he called out to Mom. "It's Tiana, and...we have company."

I walked inside with the four men trailing behind me.

"Tiana?" said my mom, dropping the spoon she was washing into the sink. She turned off the fire on the stove and slowly walked towards me. "So you're back, huh?"

"Yes," I said. I could tell she was pissed by the way her fingers were tapping on the kitchen counter. And her tone was deliberate and quiet.

"Why are you back if you wanted to leave so bad? If we were such bad parents?" she spat out.

"Bianca, don't be so hard," my dad interjected, but she wasn't having it.

My mom kept going. "You think it was easy, knowing you were on that stupid cruise and not knowing if you were alive? Do you know how it feels to lose a child? After all we've done for you.."

I couldn't take it anymore.

I opened my mouth to say something smart, but my lips trembled, and tears burst out.

"I always thought of you. Always," I said. "I wanted to come back because I missed you. I know it was crazy to leave like that, but I always felt so lonely, like I was missing something important. You can't rip something like that away from me. I felt cut off from the rest of the world taking those pills. You'll never understand."

My tears were flowing freely down my cheeks now. My mom's eyes were starting to tear up.

"I'm sorry, honey," she said. "I didn't know you felt like

that. I thought the pills made you not care about that stuff. Like dating and guys."

"It's okay," I said, finally able to breathe again.

"Just don't run away like that, okay?" she said as we hugged and she kissed my cheek.

"I won't," I said, the smell of onions strong in my nose as we hugged. When we pulled away, she looked at the men sitting quietly on the couch.

"And who are you?"

Grant shot up from his seat and shook my mom's hand. "I'm Grant, and this is my pack. We have gotten to know your daughter and tried to keep her safe as much as possible. We hope to have your blessings for your daughter to be part of our pack. The queen of our pack."

I could tell my mom was instantly charmed by his humble demeanor.

"I could see the marks on your neck, so I know you ain't waiting for my blessings," she joked, and the men laughed, unsure if she was being serious. "At least you seem like a good pack. Thank you for taking care of my daughter."

"They are good to me," I said.

"Gentlemen, please sit. I'd like to get to know you and get the latest from Howl's Edge," announced my dad.

As the guys talked, I touched my ever-growing belly. I wore a loose pink flowing shirt over my jeans to cover it.

I was super nervous about announcing my pregnancy. I wasn't sure how my parents would respond to the news. Or if they would be angry. As Grant droned on about police work to my dad, I felt happy and cozy sitting between Wesley and Sam on the couch. I felt a little dizzy and laid my head on Sam's shoulder. Tony was in the kitchen talking with my mom, and I admired the effort he was putting in. My mom wasn't too easy to talk to. But she seemed to be in good spirits as she placed the lasagna on the dining table for everyone to grab.

"Food's ready," she said.

"Ladies first," said Tony, ushering me forward. I didn't need to be asked twice. I missed my mom's cooking, and it smelled so good. I scooped a slice of the juicy goodness and made my way back into the living room, which seemed even tinier with all the alphas crowding the space.

As we ate and conversed about everything, my mom pulled me into the kitchen.

"Are you happy with this pack of alphas?" she asked me, her eyes concerned.

"I am," I replied.

"How about school? What's going to happen?"

"I want to stay in Howl's Edge for a while longer and learn where we came from," I said. I had thought about this for days and days. I wasn't happy with college here and didn't know what I was doing with my life before I met Grant and his pack. "Mom, I have something else to tell you."

"What is it?" she asked, taking a sip of the homemade juice.

"I'm pregnant," I blurted out. I was done keeping secrets and was tired of it. I touched my little belly that wasn't showing yet. She nearly choked on her drink and set it down slowly.

Her eyes were wide, and her face lit with joy.

"We're going to have a grandbaby!" she exclaimed, hugging me again. I laughed in relief. "You've already made your life choices, so there's no use regretting anything."

"I know," I said.

My dad came to congratulate me next, and I knew he was excited.

"I thought this day would never happen," he said. "Your

mother and I left Howl's Edge to protect you, and it seems things are a little safer now."

"It is," said Tony.

"I think we should go back home," my mom said to my dad.

"Home where?" asked my dad.

"Howl's Edge."

"I agree," my dad replied.

Twenty-Three

TIANA

Nine Months Later

Being nine months pregnant wasn't fun.

I felt ready to pop as I helped paint the garage in our new home in Howl's Edge.

The men wore plastic garb from head to toe, while I wore a simple black apron over my maternity clothes. It was a beautiful day outside. I could see the ocean's waves from our new house. I loved it. Grant and the pack were able to buy a house on the island after working a couple of months with Caleb, and we had just moved in.

I never imagined how big I had gotten. It was heavy carrying around this baby, but at least the nausea and dizziness stopped.

"Take a break, baby," said Wesley, coming over and kissing my neck.

"Painting takes my mind off things," I insisted, swiping the paintbrush over the wall in a neat stroke of white paint. I was enjoying this. I straightened back up, massaging my lower back.

"Your dad will have my neck if I don't stop you from working," said Wesley. "Considering that they live right next door."

"How do you feel about them living next door?" I asked lightly, knowing he was the most nervous of all the men.

"I got used to it," said Wesley, taking off his glove and rubbing my pregnant belly in circles. The men loved rubbing my belly and feeling the baby kick. We purposely didn't want to find out the gender of the baby. The doctor at the Omega Birthing Clinic said I'd have to go through a scheduled c-section as most omegas did. I didn't feel comfortable with that, but I still wanted to be alive at the end of all this.

"Wesley, quit flirting and get working," grunted Grant. "Tonight is your turn with her anyway."

"I'm trying to get her to stop working so hard," argued Wesley. Then, under his breath. "Jealous ass."

I started to feel a twinge in my lower belly, like a tightening in my lower section.

I set the paintbrush down.

"You might be right, actually," I said. "I'm going to take a little break."

"Let me get a kiss first, beautiful," said Tony.

I looked up, and his lips descended on mine. Kissing me thoroughly before I left the garage. Butterflies never failed to overwhelm me every time he kissed me like this. His sweet smell of cologne was like a drug. I felt like he and Grant were the most jealous of all the guys when it came to me.

"You smell good," I said.

He kissed my neck and tried pulling down my white shirt. My skin heated under his warm, thick lips.

"Tony, get to work," ordered Grant. "We got to get this garage done by tonight."

"Alright," he rasped, reluctantly lifting his mouth off the top of my boob.

"We'll play later," I whispered teasingly, biting his lower lip.

"Damn," he breathed as I walked away.

I was aroused right now, but I didn't want to start a fight in there. Grant and Sam seemed pretty serious this morning about getting all the painting done in the house before the new baby arrived next week.

I removed my apron and walked into the house. The house was spacious, with tall cream walls and a beige sectional in the living room. The kitchen had a large island in the middle of it, and I bought a little plant to put in the middle.

Pouring a glass of water, I stood in the kitchen, chugging it down. It felt so cool and refreshing down my throat. I took my apron off and hung it over a chair as another spasm of pain wracked through me.

I slowly limped to the closest bedroom. The baby's nursery.

I sat on the rocking chair, looking around at the finished room. We decorated the walls light green, and the little bed was covered in green sheets. I had so much fun decorating this room with my pack. Little plush fur toys were everywhere, and a giant teddy bear sat in the corner at Tony's insistence. I couldn't wait for my baby to enjoy all this.

Suddenly, a sharp pain hit my lower belly, and I groaned, holding my stomach. This felt different.

The pain intensified and tightened. That's when I realized these were serious contractions. All day I had felt little twinges here and there, but nothing this intense. I stayed hunched on the rocking chair until the pain passed.

I stood up and suddenly felt a gush between my legs.

"Oh no," I said, looking down. My black maternity sweatpants were all wet. I started to panic when another wave of contraction squeezed my belly, not releasing me. I yelled out for help. "Grant! Wesley!"

Shit, the men couldn't hear me. They were in the garage.

I stayed hunched over, and the tightening started to release.

I took off my pants and slowly made my way into the bedroom. As I was pulling on a new pair of sweatpants, another contraction seized me. This time, it made me double over in pain.

This was hard. It was too painful.

I couldn't do this.

"Grant!" I yelled louder through my pain.

***

Grant

"NICE JOB," I said, looking around at our handiwork.

The paint job was finally done. Ripping off my gloves, I thought about Tiana and wondered if she was sleeping.

"Whole house is done," said Sam, rubbing the sweat off his forehead.

"Hell yeah," said Wesley. "Should I order pizza for later?"

"Go ahead," I said, placing my body suit on the garage floor. I walked inside the house. I missed Tiana already.

I heard her call out. It sounded weak. She didn't sound alright. I began running towards the master bedroom and flung the door wide open.

She was lying on the floor of the bed, her pants half-on as she writhed in pain.

"Tiana!" I shouted, running to her. "Is it the baby?"

She nodded weakly, her face stark with fear. Her eyes were wide with shock at what her body was doing. I knew omega birthing was difficult, and I was instantly scared.

"What's going on?" said Tony rushing over.

"She's in labor. Get the car started," I said, gathering her in my arms.

"My pants," she said weakly, struggling against me.

"It's okay," I said, holding her against my chest as I ran out the door to Wesley's and Sam's shock.

"What's going on?" said Wesley.

"She's in labor," I said.

"Damn," said Sam rushing to open the van door.

Everyone piled into the van, with me holding her on my lap in the backseat. She only had on pink underwear and an oversized white shirt. She moaned in pain, her eyes closed as she squeezed my arm. We were soon speeding down the roads.

"It's okay, baby. We're almost there. Drive faster, Tony," I said.

"I am goddamn it," said Tony, pressing the gas pedal.

Tiana screamed. "I feel it down there. It's huge."

"Fuck," I said, pushing her hair back from her forehead. She was sweating, and her thighs were shaking on Sam's lap. Could she be giving birth to an alpha baby? Alpha babies were usually bigger than most.

And she was a tiny omega. So I grew even more scared- my heart beating a mile a minute.

Upon reaching the hospital, I rushed to the front desk with Tiana in my arms.

"Reason for visit?" asked the receptionist.

"She's about to give birth," I barked. *Can't these people see she was in pain?* Everyone was moving so slowly.

They rolled her on a stretcher to her room, and I followed close behind.

When we entered the room, the nurses surrounded her. They immediately hooked her up to many wires and put her in a birthing position on the bed.

I pulled my phone out and called Tiana's mother.

"Hello?"

"We're in the hospital now. The baby. The baby might be coming tonight," I said, trying not to trip over my words. My breathing was accelerated, and I was on high alert. I had to protect my pack at all costs. My omega.

I wasn't going to leave her side.

Not for a moment.

<hr>

Tiana

"Push," said the doctor, looking between my legs. The doctor was a dark-haired young woman with a serious expression with her name badge saying *Keera* on it.

I was in way too much pain to listen calmly to her.

"I need pain medicine!" I shouted.

"It's too late for that," said Dr. Keera.

My legs were in stirrups, and Grant kept wiping the sweat off my forehead with a tissue. Tony and Sam were holding my hands on either side. The pressure between my legs grew as I pushed again.

The pain was ripping through me. I howled in pain, gnashing my teeth.

"I can't do this!" I screamed.

"The baby is almost out," said Dr. Keera calmly. "Take a deep breath and push as hard as you can."

I braced myself and pressed down as hard as I could. It was like a basketball weighing down on me as I screamed.

The pain was overwhelming. Nothing I've ever felt before.

"My mom, call my mom," I gasped.

"I did," said Grant. "Keep pushing, Tiana. You're doing so good, baby."

"I can see the baby's head!" shouted Tony as he rubbed my bare thigh.

That gave me the impetus to push again. My baby was almost out. But exhaustion pressed over me.

"Your mom is here," said Grant, and relief washed over me. If I died during childbirth, she was here at least.

"Push, push, push," encouraged Dr. Keera.

Tears streamed down my face from the glaring pain. I couldn't do this.

I was close to collapsing.

"Tiana, sweetie, listen to me. Push," I heard my mom's voice in my ear. "Push Tiana."

"I can't," I said, my eyes still closed.

"Push as hard as you can. You're almost there," she said. "You can do this."

I listened to her voice. I took a deep breath and pushed again.

Then, there was a gurgle and a tiny shriek of a newborn baby.

"Good job! It's a girl, and it looks like she's an omega," said Dr. Keera, handing the baby to one of the nurses. I took in a deep breath, but something felt wrong.

The relief was short-lived before my abdomen tightened again, and I shouted in pain. The pain was happening all over again.

"Tiana is still in pain," said Grant, keen eyes observing me.

Dr. Keera peered between my legs and gasped.

"There's a second baby in there," she said. "Tiana, I want you to push immediately."

Tears continued to fall down my face. I couldn't do this again. I was out of strength.

But I knew I'd regret it if I didn't give this my all. I gritted my teeth and screamed as I pushed.

The baby's twin came out on the first push, and I

collapsed against the bed in exhaustion, laying my head against the pillow at last.

My stomach muscles started to relax, and my pain lessened immensely.

"You did it," said Grant proudly, kissing my cheek. I smiled through my exhaustion.

"This one is a baby boy! He's a big one, could be an alpha," said Dr. Keera.

After a few moments, the babies were placed on my chest. Their little bodies were warm as they squirmed on me.

My heart swelled, and I looked up at my mated pack. Wesley had his hand to his mouth. Grant had tears in his eyes, and so did Tony. Sam gently rubbed the back of one of the babies, his smile large.

"We created this," I whispered, kissing the babies as they whined and cried. I cuddled them through my exhaustion, never wanting to let them go.

After ten minutes of holding them, I handed them over.

Grant and Wesley took them from my arms as I fondly watched my mom and my alphas fuss and coo over the babies.

They were precious.

And my little family was finally complete.

THE END

Epilogue

ONE MONTH LATER

Tiana

Today was the birth celebration for the twins.

I was excited as I pulled on a shimmering white dress over my body. I had carefully chosen this dress with my mom in anticipation for this big day.

"Wes, could you help me zip up my dress?" I called. Wesley was in the bathroom doing the finishing touches on his hair.

"How do I look?" asked Wesley, stepping into the room. He wore a navy blue suit which looked sharp. And his hair was gelled back.

"You look handsome as always," I complimented. He beamed, coming up behind me, and I could feel the warmth of his body press up against me. His cock pressed into my back. In slow motion, he zipped up my dress while kissing my neck.

"You look too hot in this dress," said Wesley. "I don't know about you going out like this."

. . .

To read the rest of the **Epilogue**: https://dl.bookfunnel. com/4fgucwcgux

It will require you to sign up for my newsletter. I promise no spam. You'll only get early cover reveals, first chapter of new books when available & exclusive discounts. Enjoy the epilogue! (*a birth celebration, push gifts & lots of steamy scenes*)

Continue on reading to **BOOK 2**: Auctioned To The Pack

This next book in the series will feature omega Dr. Keera (Tiana's midwife) with the **Lustfur Pack**. Keera's father has it out for her and she's sent to the Omega Auctions. But Jatix is the one to bid the highest offer. Will she fall in love with Jatix (*with his peculiar tastes*) or go back to her abusive father?

Or jump to **Book 6** Knotted by The Pack featuring Tiana's daughter (Alana) and her search for love, although it's recommended to read the series in order for the best experience.

Also By Layla Sparks

Howl's Edge Island: Omega For The Pack (COMPLETED Reverse Harem Series)

Book 1 (*Tiana's story*): <u>Stolen by The Pack</u>

Book 2 (*Keera's story*): <u>Auctioned to the Pack</u>

Book 3 (*Lyra's story*): <u>Princess For The Pack</u>

Book 4 (*Vanessa's story*): <u>Betrayed by The Pack</u>

Book 5 (*Jade's story*): <u>Matched to The Pack</u>

Book 6 (*Alana's story*): <u>Knotted by The Pack</u>

Book 7 (*Lacy's story*): <u>Craved by The Pack</u>

Book 8 (*Olivia's story*): <u>Freed by The Pack</u>

OR grab the FULL series in one ebook here: Omega for The Pack Books 1-8

Paperback Version (containing books 1-3): Omega for The Pack 1-3

Paperback Version (books 4-6): Omega for The Pack 1-4

Paperback Version (books 7-8): Omega for The Pack 7-8

Dawn of The Alphas: Omega For The Pack Series *(spinoff of the Howl's Edge series)*

Book 1: <u>Maid for The Alphas</u>

Book 2: <u>Promised to The Alphas</u>

Book 3: <u>Denied by The Alphas</u>

Acknowledgments

Thank you for reading the first book in the Howl's Edge Island series! I really hope you enjoyed it.

Please leave a review letting me know your favorite parts of the story. This helps authors like me keep producing more stories for you.

To get updates on my next book and to get exclusive cover reveals and first chapters, sign up for my newsletter below: Newsletter